Praise for the national bestselling Suga

Drizzled with De

"*Drizzled with Death*, the first in the Suga
Jessie Crockett, reminds me of exactly why
teries so much. Hilarity ensues from the
doesn't let up, even with a murder mystery
the character of Dani. She's spunky, begui
syrup, and I can relate to all the problems sh
with her family . . . The fact that you'll pro
to guess who the killer is until the big reveal is just another
reason to get your hands on a copy, along with the delicious
maple syrup recipes you get at the end." —*Fresh Fiction*

"The mystery was well put together and had my inner ama-
teur sleuth working overtime, trying to solve it before
Dani. I was in suspense, right up until the end, while I
watched the mystery unravel before me . . . Dani and her
family were a hoot and I can't wait to see what trouble Dani
is going to get into next!" —*Cozy Mystery Book Reviews*

"It's a hysterical tale of maple syrup and mayhem set
against the backdrop of the New England leaves . . . This
book had me snickering from the first chapter. Author
Jessie Crockett has a knack for writing comedy into her
mysteries . . . The mystery aspect . . . was just as funny as
the rest of it. There were so many suspects and a plethora
of motives, but Crockett easily keeps the readers guessing
all the way to the end." —*Debbie's Book Bag*

"[A] light, fun mystery with colorful characters, the major-
ity of whom seem to be keeping secrets. Dani Greene was
an enjoyable character with a lot of spunk."
—*Once Upon a Romance*

Berkley Prime Crime titles by Jessie Crockett

DRIZZLED WITH DEATH
MAPLE MAYHEM
A STICKY SITUATION

A
Sticky
SITUATION

Jessie Crockett

BERKLEY PRIME CRIME, NEW YORK

THE BERKLEY PUBLISHING GROUP
Published by the Penguin Group
Penguin Group (USA) LLC
375 Hudson Street, New York, New York 10014

USA • Canada • UK • Ireland • Australia • New Zealand • India • South Africa • China

penguin.com

A Penguin Random House Company

A STICKY SITUATION

A Berkley Prime Crime Book / published by arrangement with the author

For information, address: The Berkley Publishing Group,
a division of Penguin Group (USA) LLC,
375 Hudson Street, New York, New York 10014.

ISBN: 978-0-425-26021-0   5550 7239

PUBLISHING HISTORY
Berkley Prime Crime mass-market edition / April 2015   4/15

PRINTED IN THE UNITED STATES OF AMERICA

10 9 8 7 6 5 4 3 2 1

Cover illustration by Mary Ann Lasher.
Interior text design by Kelly Lipovich.

Acknowledgments

Writing this book has been a pleasure and a privilege. Several people have helped to make it even more so. I'd like to thank my agent, John Talbot; my editor, Michelle Vega; cover artist Mary Ann Lasher-Dodge; and all the people at Berkley Prime Crime who make everything work behind the scenes. A big thank-you also goes out to the nice guys at Sap House Meadery in Center Ossipee, New Hampshire, for answering questions and providing inspiration.

I am also very fortunate to have support in my personal life for my endeavors. My fellow Wicked Cozy authors, Sherry Harris, J. A. Hennrikus, Edith Maxwell, Liz Mugavero, and Barbara Ross have been an invaluable group of traveling companions on the writing journey. I don't know what I'd do without all of you!

I am so grateful to be blessed with enthusiastic encouragement from my mother, Sandy Crockett, and my sisters,

Acknowledgments

Larissa Crockett and Barb Shaffer. I'm also so appreciative of the endless patience and staunch support shown by my children.

And lastly, I want to thank my husband, Elias Estevao, the hero at the heart of all my stories.

One

 I knew there was trouble when Celadon sought me out in the sugar bush. Usually she sends one of her children to find me in the woods, preferring her fuzzy slippers to snow boots. My sister is generally considered a handsome woman but this could not be said as she waddled toward me through the snow. She knows to use snowshoes but in her haste must have forgotten them. Her earmuffs lopsidedly clung to her head for dear life and her scarf dragged behind her like a leash that lost its dog. By the time she got to me she was out of breath and had to reach out her hands to steady herself on a tree. Just looking at her I felt panic rising.

"Who's hurt?" I imagined my grandfather slumped in his chair, something vital burst in his brain or my brother, Loden, clutching at a hand short a couple of fingers. Celadon shook her head.

"Hazel." And with that one word the joy sucked out of my day like the air from a plane in a suspense movie when a mad bomber blows a hole in the side. As a sugar maker, I love the early spring. Those four to six weeks every year when the days are relatively warm and the nights are still cold. My whole family waits for this period when the sap runs like most families anticipate an annual vacation at a beach house. And when I say the whole family, I mean the whole family.

The Greene family is a big one and has a vast array of members, most of whom manage to find their way back to Sugar Grove at some point while the sap is running. You can never be sure when Aunt Peridot or Cousin Moss will descend on us but you know it will happen. Like flu season, its course trends and you note the signs with trepidation. But my grandfather's sister Hazel and her granddaughter Jade were sure to appear every year in time for the Sugar Grove Maple Festival. Their exact arrival date is always a surprise but they never fail to be around for the festival weekend.

The festival is the highlight of the year in town and so naturally, that was when they would visit. It was more fun and less work and for all the years her age was right, Jade entered and won the Miss Maple competition. Now that she is beyond competition age and runs her own pageant coaching business she still makes time to come every year. Her days as Miss Maple may be behind her but she still reminds us every time we see her that she won over and over and Celadon and I never even entered.

"When?"

"She'll be here in fifteen minutes. She hired a car to drive her up." Of course she did. I wasn't sure why she came every year to participate in sugaring since it is, at its heart, a do-it-yourself kind of thing. Our aunt has a policy of never doing for yourself what you can get others to do for you and she has taught her granddaughter to approach life in the same manner. It would never occur to any of the rest of us to hire a car. There's a perfectly good bus that runs from Boston to Concord, NH, where any one of us would have unhappily picked them up from the station. But Hazel didn't like public transport and nothing was ever good enough for her granddaughter Jade, as she was quick to point out to anyone within earshot.

"Did you think to grab some car keys on your way out?"

"Of course."

We crept to the back of the barn and Celadon silently gestured to the family minivan. She slid into the passenger seat. I expected her to want to drive since she prefers to be in charge of everything but I took the keys and started the engine. I decided to risk the noise it might make and gunned the engine, tearing down the driveway and setting a personal best in terms of speed.

Grandma might have been standing on the porch waving her arms at us but I won't swear to it. I hated leaving her in the lurch knowing full well she'd feel obliged to put on a big dinner for Hazel and Jade but desperate times called for desperate measures. Besides, our brother, Loden, never seemed to mind Hazel's company anywhere near as much as we did, so he could help Grandma out if she needed it.

"Have you turned off your cell phone?" I asked as I braked hard and swung us out onto the main road.

"I can't do that. What if the school calls because one of the kids is sick?"

"Then switch off the ringer at least. We can't have anyone at the Stack telling the family we ignored calls," I said. Celadon dug in her purse and fiddled with her phone.

"There is a bit of good news," Celadon said.

"How can there possibly be good news when Hazel and Jade arrive?"

"That's just it. Jade isn't arriving."

"What do you mean, 'isn't arriving'?"

"I mean, when Grandma asked what Jade might like for supper Hazel said Jade wasn't with her."

"But Jade always comes with her."

You know how every member of a family seems to have a role to play and no matter how old you all get, how far from your roots, you never quite shake it off? Our cousin Jade's role is to be the one thing Celadon and I ever entirely agree upon. We both wish she didn't exist. Summers when we were kids involved extended doses of Jade. Her parents worried she needed more interaction with her cousins since she was an only child and they felt long bouts of time with us was the answer.

They weren't particularly interested in her developing

better social skills; they wanted her to stop asking them for a sibling. After all, how likely would it be for them to produce a second perfect child? They were sticking with one and that was that. Jade not visiting was the best news I'd had in a long time.

"Maybe after what happened last year she decided it would be best not to come." Celadon dug her long fingers into my arm. "You do remember the visit last year?" Celadon's breath was coming in shallow pants and her cheeks flushed like a male cardinal.

"How could I forget?" Last year, when Celadon's daughter was five, Jade decided she had found her heir to the Miss Maple throne. She snuck Spring off for a day of beauty and returned with a miniaturized version of herself: high heels, clingy short dress, bubble gum pink lipstick, and a generous squirt of a heady fragrance unfortunately named Every Man's Desire wafting from her tiny body. Jade had registered her for the competition, purchased her competition wardrobe, and schooled her in a routine involving a striptease down to a polka-dotted bikini without asking Celadon's permission for any of it.

When chided for her actions she asked if Celadon really wanted her daughter to turn out like me. Spring was overwrought by the whole experience and tugged in two directions by a pair of emotional powerhouses; she locked herself in the bathroom where she announced through the keyhole she planned to eat toothpaste to stay alive until the fighting stopped. It was a low point for us all.

Then I had another thought that burst my bliss bubble before it really had a chance to inflate.

"What will Hazel do if she doesn't have Jade to focus on? Will she turn all that attention on us?"

"It doesn't bear thinking about."

The Stack was still serving the breakfast crowd when we walked in, and heads turned to see both of us there together. Celadon is the old-fashioned sort of woman who dresses to go to town and to see her standing there with her hair straggling out and her pant legs soaked to mid-thigh was a first for most of the patrons. The Stack Shack is always busy in the morning but there was an even bigger crowd than usual gathered around the counter, coffee mugs clutched tightly in work-hardened hands. The chatter was unusually loud, too.

Instead of grabbing a stool at the counter I steered Celadon to my favorite booth in the back. Before long Piper hustled up with a sparkling coffeepot and some questions.

"Is it Hazel or Jade?" she asked, flipping the mugs upright and filling them with a practiced flick of the wrist.

"What makes you ask that?" Celadon said, gripping the mug in her two hands like it was Jade's perfect, lily-white neck.

"Every sugaring season the two of you burst in here like a couple of escaped convicts, your eyes lolling and furtively darting. If I didn't know you I would have phoned the police before your butts hit these seats. The only thing I know that rattles both of you that much is the arrival of your great-aunt and her offspring."

"It's just Hazel. Jade isn't with her."

"That's one more thing to set tongues wagging," Piper said.

"It does seem especially lively in here this morning. Is something going on?"

"You know that old building someone's been fixing up at the end of Church Street?"

"The one that used to be a general store?" The building had been a general store for years before the Mountain View Food Mart set up in town. Over the years it had languished and when the last owners died no one had wanted to keep running the place as a store. The space was large but not really large enough for a grocer and the town wasn't big enough to support two grocery stores anyway. Parking was a problem, too. And the septic wasn't built for heavy use so converting the building to apartments wasn't even an option.

It sat and sat, growing more depressing each year. Everyone said something ought to be done about it and we all felt guilty over what was becoming of the place. Grampa had mentioned buying it but Grandma had nixed that idea pretty quickly. She said he was already spreading himself too thin and the projects that really had his heart would suffer for it. So it continued to sit vacant, chiding us all.

"That's the one."

"What about it?"

"There's a sign on the front of the building saying that the work is almost done and that the owner will be unveiling it tomorrow afternoon."

"You're kidding." No wonder there was a buzz of

excitement. For months hammering and banging could be heard almost constantly from inside the building. The windows were all covered over with newspaper and the crew hustling in and out couldn't be convinced to say a thing. And believe me, people had tried. According to Myra Phelps, police dispatcher and gossip extraordinaire, the property had been purchased by a corporation that didn't seem to be connected to the town in any way. None of the names she'd been able to track down looked familiar and the purpose for the purchase remained shrouded in mystery.

"I want to know who snatched away the best contractor in town." I had hoped Wesley Farnum would be available to start the work on the opera house project but the mystery owner of the building booked him first and he had been right out straight ever since.

"We'll finally find out who's responsible for the Russ Collins situation," Celadon said. We had been forced to hire Russ to get the project at the opera house started when the pipes in the building froze and we couldn't delay work any longer. Russ was usually available since he paced himself like an arthritic inchworm. On the plus side he was a gifted storyteller. I had heard more creative excuses for why so little had been done clearing the coal room in the cellar of the town hall than I could have imagined possible. I'm used to Grampa and his embellishment of favorite stories but Russ had missed his calling. He would have been a champion wandering bard, raking in the coins for singing exaggerated praises of the local big cheese. Well, if he could get motivated enough to wander away from a soft bed and a hot meal.

"I'll be glad when Wesley is freed up and able to work on something new." I had ended up being the point of contact for Russ. Celadon's strategy for suffering fools was to put them out of their misery. Not without reason Grandma had asked me to deal with Russ until the job was complete since she didn't want the family ending up in the papers on account of any violence. Celadon had sensitive skin and would never be able to endure the soap in the county lockup.

"Why don't you put those menus away? I'll be right back with just what you need to take your mind off all your troubles, family or community." Piper hurried off and returned just a moment later, placing an overflowing vintage dessert bowl, the cut glass ones with the feet, in front of each of us.

"What is it?" I asked, lifting a spoon in anticipation.

"Chocolate cherry lava cups." Piper nodded and smiled. "Nothing like chocolate and cherries and cake to fix what ails you. Let me know what you think" She headed toward the door as a new set of customers entered the Stack. I stuck my spoon down through the gooey layers of chocolaty goodness. Lifting it to my mouth I spotted cherry preserves, hot fudge, and chunks of chocolate cake. Divine. Even Celadon seemed to be simmering down. Maybe she would be lulled into a sugar stupor and forget.

"This is incredible." Celadon forgot herself enough

to dribble fudge sauce down her chin. "Piper is an amazing cook. Maybe we should just stay here."

"How would we get away with that? Everyone will see us in here and report back to the family."

"Maybe we could get Mitch to arrest us. I'm sure you could do something that upsets him enough to get us thrown in jail for a few days."

"I don't think that will work anymore. At least not as long as he is still dating Phoebe." Mitch was a local cop and my former boyfriend. He had been ruthlessly harassing me for the last few months. That is until he started dating Phoebe Jones and his obsession with me began to cause friction in their relationship. I hadn't gotten so much as a parking ticket or jaywalking fine in weeks.

"Knowlton would help us, wouldn't he?" Celadon asked, dabbing at the chocolate on her chin with a paper napkin, her hand shaking.

"Even Hazel and Jade combined don't make me that desperate."

"We could bribe Doc MacIntyre to say we both had come down with something that requires us to be quarantined. Then we could skip town until Hazel leaves."

"You don't mean Yahtzee."

"It's the only way. We'd have to agree to be his Yahtzee slaves until he died." The local doctor was a great all-around guy. He was an old-fashioned country doctor who birthed babies and eased the suffering of the very elderly. He even still made house calls. But you didn't want to be without an excuse to avoid playing Yahtzee with him. The guy had made the *Guinness*

Book of Records for the longest continual game of Yahtzee ever played. All he had to do was hear the slightest rattle in your lungs during an exam and he couldn't focus on his job until he told you all about his latest game. People had been known to pay their doctor bills in Yahtzee pads. It should have been funny but it was sort of terrifying instead.

"I don't think we will get away with it. Not unless we are actually incapacitated. You know Grandma would insist on taking care of us herself." A shadow fell over the table and we both jumped. I looked up to see my godfather, Lowell, towering over us, his uniform freshly pressed and his gun sitting snugly in its holster just about at my eye level.

"And who is helping to take care of your grand-mother? You know how hard on her Hazel's visits always are." Celadon and I both slid low in our benches, the guilt of leaving Grandma on her own to deal with Hazel making us hang our heads in shame. "I know just as soon as you two finish up your food you'll do the right thing and head on home. Even if it takes a police escort to get you to do it."

Lowell was just about the easiest-going guy I had ever met but he took all his duties seriously. That included policing the community as well as serving as a surrogate son to my grandparents ever since my father died several years ago. There was no way we could put off our responsibilities with him around to remind us of them.

Two

We bumped on down the driveway. Celadon had come back to her senses enough to want to be the one behind the wheel. She didn't slow a bit as she wheeled into the dirt track leading up to Greener Pastures. The time of year was perfect to begin sugaring. The fluctuating day and nighttime temperatures made the sap in the maple trees begin to flow and harvesting it became possible. It had a less useful effect on the driveway. Every day a crop of fresh ruts appeared on the driveway where thawing made mud appear. Tires moving up and down throughout the day made gouges which froze in solid and inconvenient lumps by late afternoon.

As soon as the sun began to dip below the rise, blobs of mud churned up through the course of the day froze into jagged peaks like a miniature mountain range in the driveway making it treacherous to navigate all evening and into the early morning hours. Celadon didn't even appear to notice as she dove up and down their peaks and valleys and even skimmed across the tops of several.

Celadon bolted from the van and headed for a little-used side door in an effort to avoid Hazel for as long as possible. I would have followed her example except for the fact I spotted Graham's state-issued truck in the yard. I had met the good-looking conservation officer back in November when he had been in Sugar Grove on business for the Fish and Game Department. Over the last few months we had gone on a number of dates and were starting to feel like a couple. My heart gave a little thump and a squishy lurch and the urge to see him outweighed the desire to avoid Hazel.

I stepped into the hall and listened for voices. Not surprisingly the sounds of chatting drifted toward me from the kitchen. Bracing myself for possible Hazel impact I followed the sounds. I paused out of sight just beyond the door to listen for Graham's voice. There was no way I was going in there with Hazel if he was not there, too.

"So, big feller, you look like quite the strapping young buck. Too bad it's not rutting season. I could teach you a thing or two, I expect." Hazel had a penchant for men, mostly the younger variety. If I didn't interfere she would drag him to her room and truss him to a bedpost before he knew what had happened to him. There was no time to waste lurking about in the hall. I gathered up my courage and stepped into the kitchen.

"Aunt Hazel, what a surprise," I said, crossing the room to give her an expected peck on the cheek. She wore her usual getup of a menswear-inspired pantsuit and a fedora. She looked like something out of a hard-boiled detective novel, right down to the tumbler of whiskey clutched in her hand. Graham looked more like a bug caught in a jar. If a bug could have a pleading look in its eyes.

"Well, it shouldn't be. I always arrive in time for maple festival. Not the brightest star in the night sky, is she, Graham?" That was Hazel, in a nutshell. She made it impossible to like her. Responding only makes things worse. It was always best to just move on and pretend you didn't hear. I turned my attention to Graham, will-ing him to understand just by the way I wiggled my eyebrows that he didn't need to answer. Apparently he doesn't speak eyebrow.

"I can't agree with you there, ma'am. Dani's got enough sparkle in her to light up my life." I couldn't believe it. That guy was just adorable. And about to be eaten alive by a rabid octogenarian.

"Is that right? And you looked like someone with high standards. Now if you wanted to pair off with one of the girls in this family you ought to hold out for my granddaughter Jade. She's learned everything she knows about men from me." Hazel downed a swig of her whis-key. Interactions with Hazel were never improved by her being a bit lit. It just made her speak more boldly. Which is to say it was a bit like stretching a giraffe's neck. I tried wresting control of the conversation.

"I wasn't expecting to see you today, Graham. What brings you by?"

"I was up this way on a call which took less time than I'd have expected. I wondered if you'd like to go to lunch with me?"

"Good thinking, young man. A body could starve around here. I mean, just look at Dani. No meat on her bones and stunted to boot. Where are you taking us?" Hazel swallowed another gulp of whiskey and winked at Graham, who took a step backward and braced his hand against the counter behind him.

"I'm sorry, ma'am, but I've brought my state-issued truck. With all the equipment I have to carry there is really only room for myself and one passenger."

"I'm starved. Let's leave right now." Just as I grabbed his arm my cell phone rang. I didn't want to answer but I couldn't seem to let myself ignore it. You know how some people can't stop reading a book they hate because they feel like they have to finish every one they start? I feel that same sort of compulsion about a ringing phone. It has to be answered.

It was Russ Collins. I reminded myself to use a polite voice when answering. There was nothing to say that Russ was calling just to get out of working. I took a couple of deep, cleansing breaths then pressed the answer button.

"Dani, I've had to stop working." Russ sounded like he was taking a few deep breaths himself. Which was something I had never heard him do before.

"Let me guess, you broke the handle to the shovel

and need to stop work to go buy a new one? No worries, I was just heading out so I'll bring one to you."

"I don't need a new shovel but I do need you to get over here ASAP."

"Russ, I'm just about to go to lunch. Unless you give me a crazy-good reason for quitting I suggest you wait until I finish my meal."

"I can't tell you on the phone. You wouldn't believe me. If you're not here in under half an hour you'll be hearing about this on the news and I'll be suing you."

"Suing me? For what?"

"Undisclosed hazardous working conditions. Or something like that. Loden would know what I could bring for charges."

"Loden isn't going to help you figure out how to sue his own family." At least I didn't think he would. He gets along with all of us better than anyone else does. But he does love a good legal puzzle. I decided it was better not to find out if his loyalties would withstand his flirtation with the law. Besides, I was sort of curious as to what Russ would consider hazardous. Spiders maybe. Or a lack of sunlight in the basement that could lead to a vitamin D deficiency perhaps.

"I'll be over just as soon as I can get there." I disconnected and turned to Graham. "I'm so sorry. Russ Collins has hit some sort of snag at the opera house. Can I have a rain check?"

"Of course. It was a long shot anyway since I know how busy you must be at this time of year." He reached out and gave my hand a squeeze. I hurried out of the room and was halfway down the hall when I heard Hazel pipe up again.

"Well, young man, it looks like you've found room in your truck for me after all. I'll just fetch my coat."

Over the few years of our acquaintance I had many times wished I had never had to interact with Russ Collins. I certainly had never wanted to drop operations at Greener Pastures during the busy season to get to the bottom of why he wasn't doing what he was paid to be doing. I regretted more than ever agreeing to hire him for the work Greener Pastures was helping to subsidize on the opera house restoration.

For the past several years the good people of Sugar Grove had been hosting and supporting fund-raisers to restore the opera house to its former glory. Just last month the committee had run Meat Bingo, one of the most popular fund-raisers in town, to try to bulk up the coffers. Finally, an anonymous donor, also known as my grandparents, had come up with sufficient funds to get the first part of the renovations under way.

An early February cold snap had frozen and burst a few pipes in the ancient heating system and Grampa felt if we waited any longer for the money to trickle in through the usual fund-raising routes the opera house would rot off before summer. He told my grandmother he wanted to sit in the balcony and neck with her in the dark once more before they both died and he didn't see that happening without a little help.

Which meant the restoration committee, composed of my grandparents, my sister, Celadon, Doc MacIntyre, the fire chief, Cliff Thompson, and yours truly got on the stick and hired Russ to begin the grunt work in the basement for a new heating system. Russ wasn't really skilled at much except coming up with excuses for not working, but skilled labor wasn't what we needed.

The old coal room in the basement still had some leftover coal in it that needed clearing out to make room for the high-efficiency unit we were installing for the whole building. The town hall would get the benefit of the upgrade as well and the whole town would enjoy decreased heating costs in their tax bills while simultaneously restoring heat to the subzero opera house.

Why I had to be the only Greene in the house when Russ called to say he had run into a problem I couldn't imagine. Sure, I was the only one whose stomach was growling only a couple hours after breakfast. I wondered if I had angered Mother Nature during the winter and she was making sure I wasn't going to get my hands on any maple goodness.

I tried to put Russ off but he was insistent that I drop everything and head straight over to the town hall basement. He sounded all worked up, which, knowing Russ, really was troubling. Since Russ was the only person I'd ever met who sat down to play boccie this seemed extreme.

I grumbled all the way into town. The roads were pocked with potholes and snowmelt flowed across them like the ocean waves of an incoming tide. My MG Midget was just back from its most recent emergency trip to the auto body shop and I was in no hurry to bottom it out in a rut bigger than an inground pool.

Winter in New Hampshire can be a lot of fun but the roads are generally not for the faint of heart or the low of chassis. I should have taken the farm truck or the minivan but I had missed my little car so much while it was being repaired I hated not to drive it. I always felt like I was cheating on it when I went out with any other cars.

Fortunately, parking in Sugar Grove is never a problem anytime except during maple festival weekend and I found a spot right in front of the town hall. I hustled into the building and raced for the stairs to the basement.

"Russ, where are you?" I called out. The light level in the cellar was about what you'd expect from a space with bare bulbs hanging every ten feet or so. The electrical system could use some work, too, from the looks of things. I heard some shuffling at the back where the coal storage had been so I headed in that direction.

"Back here, Dani. Did you bring a flashlight?" I pulled up short at the entrance to the coal room.

"Nope. You said hurry so I left with nothing but my car keys and a coat. I've got my cell phone we could use." I scrolled through the apps and turned on the flashlight. I swooped it around over my head and into the corners. A small amount of the leftover coal we had asked Russ to clear glinted up at me from a rusty wheelbarrow. Most of the room looked like it had the last time I had been down there with Grampa telling Russ what the job would entail. I wasn't surprised by his lack of progress but it didn't do much for my mood.

"Shine it over there." Russ pointed a grubby hand at the one bare patch in the pile of coal. I tilted the phone to where he directed and leaned in. And then drew back. And then leaned in again. I had been prepared to give Russ a piece of my mind for dragging me away from my work and my lunch with Graham. But I wasn't prepared for what he found.

"Is this a joke?"

"I was going to ask you the same thing." There was no doubt about it. Russ, despite a desire to never do a lick of work, had managed to dig up some pieces of what looked like a human skeleton. There it was, plain as day poking up from the dirt floor of the town hall cellar.

A long bone that looked to my untrained eye like it used to be in someone's leg showed nearest me. The top portion of a skull sat closer to Russ. The dome of it gleamed a bit despite the low light and the coal dust. I moved closer, bent over it, and covered my hand with the sleeve of my sweatshirt. I brushed a bit more dirt away from the area and revealed more of the skull. I was no expert but if it was a fake it was a pretty convincing one.

"How did you find this?" I asked, sinking onto the floor.

"I was just shoveling off the coal in this one area and when I scraped against the dirt floor scooping up the last bits I must have gouged the floor. You told me to be thorough so I was trying to get every bit."

"And then what?"

"And then I felt the shovel clunk into something more resistant to scooping than the coal. I gave it a harder shove but it didn't seem to matter."

"Have you called Lowell?" Lowell Matthews was the chief of police and my godfather. He was also dating my widowed mother. It was complicated but we were getting used to it.

"No."

"Why the heck did you call me instead of the police? I'm no dead-body expert." Although, lately it was beginning to feel like I was. In the last four months I'd seen more than my fair share of corpses.

"I figured if I called the police in they'd make me stop working on this job. You'd be aggravated at me for the delay. I wanted you to be the one to make the call so you and your grandfather couldn't blame me for whatever happened here." Russ sounded quarrelsome and like he had an attitude but if I looked at myself clearly I could see his point.

I might not have come right out and accused him of finding a way to get out of the work but I am certain I would have thought it. After all, that was the reputation the guy had and it was deserved. Still, it rankled to think I had a reputation of my own and it was one of being judgmental and unfair.

"You're probably right but we had best call the police now. This looks too real to ignore." I walked carefully back out of the cellar and up to the ground floor of the building. Most of the town offices in Sugar Grove are conveniently housed in the same place. If you want to speak to the tax collector, town clerk, or any selectperson happening to keep office hours you just need to hang around the town hall for a bit. They'll be around eventually.

Unfortunately, the police department is housed in a building of its own. Fortunately, it is just up the street. Within five minutes of my call Lowell and my ex-boyfriend Mitch were squatting over the partially unearthed skull, snapping pictures and speculating.

"It's pretty strange that you ended up striking this with so little work done, isn't it?" Mitch sounded like he was on a tear, already looking for someone to blame for what had happened. I didn't like Russ but there was no reason to think he had anything to do with the body other than being the poor guy who came upon it. I mean, who'd want to find a buried body anyway but certainly no one would if they were alone in a gloomy basement and the body in question was reduced to skeletal remains.

"I hardly think he would have called you if he was up to no good, Mitch. He was digging it up, not burying it."

"And what are you doing here, Dani? I can't seem to think you're much good with the heavy lifting." Which was unfair. I may weigh 103 pounds soaking wet but I can certainly hold my own when it comes to physical labor. What I lack in strength I make up for in willingness to just keep at it until the job is complete. Which is mostly why I don't respect Russ.

"I called her so she wouldn't complain I'd cut out of work early. You know how she is." Russ gave Mitch one of those man-to-man looks that mean women are a pain in the butt. Mitch nodded in agreement. That sort of thing was just one of many reasons we weren't still dating.

"Sounds reasonable." Mitch just had to contribute his two cents. Lowell stood up and crossed his arms over his chest.

"Thanks for calling us in. I think it's safe to say there is no more work for you to do here today, Russ. Why don't you head on out. I'd appreciate it if you wouldn't mention this to anyone just yet."

"I won't." Russ tugged at his ball cap and shuffled out.

"Dani, I think you'd best tell Emerald the work on the opera house is at a standstill for the time being. You can tell him why but ask the family to be discreet, please."

"Grampa isn't going to be pleased to hear this. You know how he is when he gets all worked up about a project."

"I think he'll understand. We're going to work this as a crime scene until we discover for some reason it isn't, so even if he doesn't, he'll have to live with it." Lowell was a lifelong family friend. Telling my grandfather to like it or lump it was not going to be easy for him. Especially since Grampa was the closest thing Lowell had to a father since his own parents had died in a house fire when he was a young man.

"I'll tell him. Maybe he'll be so pleased not to have to pay Russ to excavate the coal room that he'll forget all about the schedule." A girl can hope, can't she?

Three

I was wiped out. Not only was there too much on my plate, there was no food in my stomach. A lot of people might have been put off from eating by the sight of a skeleton in a basement but I figured the poor guy didn't care. Just because he was long past his last meal didn't mean I should be, too. I left the car where it was and crossed the street for the Stack Shack. Besides, I figured the Stack was probably where Graham and Hazel would be having lunch. Leaving him to fend for himself with her was not the best way to keep him around.

Coffee and bacon and cinnamon roll smells filled the air but there was no sign of Graham or Hazel. The only person in the place besides Russ and Tansey was Piper. Even the cook seemed to have taken a break. Russ perched on a stool next to Tansey, gesturing more animatedly than I had ever seen. His back was to me and he didn't notice my arrival.

Usually, anyone in the Stack swivels in their seat to get a look at new arrivals and to say hello if they're a mind to but not this time. Both Tansey and Piper were straining toward Russ. He had their full attention like nothing I'd ever seen. They looked like kids round a campfire listening to a ghost story. Tansey especially had her ears a-flapping. Both her hands wrapped round her coffee cup and she was holding the thing halfway to her mouth but had forgotten to take it to her lips.

"So I scraped away a bit more and there was a long whitish thing kinda bright against all the dirt and the coal dust. I bent over and scratched at it with my work glove."

"What was it, Russ?" Piper asked. "What did you see?"

"It was a bone. A human leg bone." Piper gasped and then pulled back as if she'd been hit with a live electrical wire.

"What made you sure it was a human bone? Couldn't it have been a dog bone or a cow bone or something like that? Couldn't it have been left from some pastureland before the town hall was built?" Tansey crossed her arms across her chest and looked smug.

"Well, I thought the same thing at first. I didn't want to get all lathered up over nothing so I thought I'd check a bit more before calling the Greenes. You know what a tartar that Dani can be." I was relieved not to see Piper's head nod in agreement. "So I poked around a bit more and eventually found another bit that confirmed my worst fears."

"Which was?" Tansey asked.

"A human skull. About the right size for a grown man, I'd say. Explain that, why don't you?" Russ looked at Tansey.

"Did you find anything else? Anything to suggest the identity of the body or how long it's been there?" Piper asked. Piper may look like a rebellious teenager with her purple hair and her multitude of tattoos but she is really one of the most practical people I know. Leave it to her to ask the pertinent questions.

"The leg bone and the skull were all I needed to see to know I wasn't the right guy for that job." Not that Russ seemed to be the right guy for any job other than potato chip taster but that was just one woman's opinion. "Now you mention it, there was one other thing I found just before I unearthed the leg bone." Russ reached into his pocket and pulled something out which he slapped on the counter with a clank. I stepped forward for a look. Everyone else leaned in, too, and then Tansey gave a little squeak, slid off her stool, and fainted dead away on the floor.

It took all of two minutes for the ambulance to arrive and whisk Tansey away. I was glad I wasn't going to be involved in explaining to her that the ambulance had been called. Tansey prided herself on her health and the thought of a public collapse was bound to wound her pride. Not to mention what the cost of an ambulance ride would do to her wallet. Not that Tansey's financials were any of my business but I knew she didn't have much to spare.

Russ had cleared out as soon as Tansey hit the floor. I wasn't sure if it was because he thought he would be blamed for upsetting her or if he thought he'd be asked to help with the stretcher. In his haste he had left his findings on the counter. Piper had sensibly not pointed this out to him as he exited. Everyone else had been so focused on Tansey that she was able to stick the items under the counter until we could speak privately.

Within minutes of Tansey being hauled away the fervor had died down and Piper retrieved Russ's objects, placing them on the counter atop a paper napkin. After all, a health inspector could drop by at any minute.

"Spoons?" I asked, scratching at the coal dust and dirt encrusting one of them.

"Looks like it. Why on earth would Tansey get so worked up about spoons?" Piper wondered.

"They don't look particularly valuable. Not silver or anything. They just look like ordinary spoons to me."

"Me, too. They don't look new but they aren't antiques I shouldn't think. I'd call them vintage." And Piper should know. She was a collector of all things vintage. Whenever she got a spare moment from the Stack, which wasn't often, she loved nothing more than a ramble through a local flea market or garage sale look-ing for more vintage kitsch to decorate either the Stack Shack or her RV. Piper loved vintage with a passion that outshone all her other loves. She wore vintage waitress uniforms and wore her purple hair in complicated styles of years gone by.

The walls of the Stack were covered in old board games, posters from classic movies, and framed baby clothes from long ago. The dishware at the Stack was vintage, too. From the juice glasses to the water tumblers, she had gathered up enough odds and ends to make the place feel like it was the resting grounds of a thousand grandmothers' kitchens. It was utterly charming.

"So what are vintage spoons doing in the town hall basement and why would they upset Tansey so much?"

"Why are there two of them? Why would they be with a body? Were they really with the body or was it a coincidence?" Piper looked over at the door as a new flood of customers flowed in. "I've got to get back to work. If I hear anything about the mystery spoons I'll let you know." Piper wrapped them in the napkin and handed them to me. "I wouldn't want these to get mixed up with mine."

"I think I'd better get these right over to Lowell. He ought to include them in whatever it is he is doing for an investigation." Piper nodded. I headed back out the door without a single morsel having passed my lips but I had a mission and didn't want to be delayed. I ignored the rumbles from my stomach as they shook my entire frame and walked the block and a half to the police station.

Housed in a small building near the center of town, the police station is one of the prettiest buildings in Sugar Grove. In the summer the window boxes spill heaps of flowers on either side of the main entrance and the butterflies and hummingbirds seem drawn to the place. When we were dating, Mitch had grumbled a bit about the station looking more like a quilt shop than a place to investigate crime. He had a point but since crime never worked up the energy to be a wave around here it hardly mattered.

Myra Phelps, the police dispatcher and all-around bearer of gossip, manned the front desk. As usual, she got right down to business.

"Tansey collapsing, what a to-do. I always said that woman's diet of fried eggs and bacon grease was going to catch up with her one day. But to do it just as the sugaring season starts, well, I can't imagine her bad luck. Poor thing. And a body in the basement of the town hall. What a morning we've been having." Myra leaned toward me, her eyes gleaming with anticipation. Did I have anything to add to her knowledge bank? Anything worth getting on the horn to her cousin in the next town about? No, I did not. There was no way I was going to link the spoons with Tansey's collapse if Myra hadn't heard about it. And I certainly wasn't going to let her know about the spoons being near the body before Lowell got the chance to hear about them. Even telling Mitch first would be preferable.

"I'm sure she'll be right as rain in no time. Tansey has a lot of bounce. Maybe she just stood up too quickly. People at the Stack were saying the body is probably left from a burial ground the town fathers didn't know about when they built the town hall, nothing more sinister than that." Myra sank back in her chair, all anticipation wiped from her face.

"Well, what can I help you with this morning?"

"Lowell isn't back from the town hall yet, is he?" I tightened my hand on the strap of my purse, feeling like Myra could guess there was something interesting in there.

"Nope. He's still over there as far as I know. Maybe if you just tell my why you're here I can give him a message."

"I'll check back later." I waved at Myra and made my escape. I walked slowly past the town hall and I thought about going back in, I really did. But when I caught sight of Mitch stringing yellow crime scene tape across the front door of the building I convinced myself to wait until later to tell Lowell about the spoons. He had to be busy and I just wasn't up for a confrontation with Mitch. Besides, I told myself, Grampa needed to hear about what had happened. As the chair of the restoration committee he needed to know that the project was going to be on hold for a bit and if I didn't get on home to tell him, someone else in town surely would.

Four

I found Grampa out in the sugar bush looking at tubing strung from tree to tree. His gnarled hands were giving it a little squeeze like he still wasn't quite sure of what he was seeing. The family had been resistant to the idea of changing to tubing for moving the sap to the sugarhouse and the evaporator but the increased efficiency had thoroughly won over everyone except Grampa. I think he missed the old way.

"Well, Dani, your newfangled tubes sure don't look too pretty weaving their way through the woods but they do hold a lot of sap."

"I know you miss the buckets and the horses carrying the sap back for us. But we can make so much more syrup this way and that benefits all the causes we support. You know that better than I do." Which he did.

Our family has money and a lot of it. I'm not bragging, it's just a fact like I'm short and my mother is a bit kooky. Since we have had far more than we need for longer than anyone can remember, we give to charities. Our initial wealth came from land ownership and it is to land trust and environmental causes that we give the most.

Everyone in the family has charities they support the most enthusiastically. Mine are environmental ones. My dream for increased production was to have more money to contribute to environmental innovations of all sorts. All post-tax profits from Greener Pastures' sugarhouse went to those causes and Grampa had always been right on board with that even when he grumbled about the way I increased the profit margin.

"Don't pay me any mind, kiddo. I'm just feeling nostalgic. It goes without saying I miss your father most at sugaring season." Grampa pulled a handkerchief out of his back pocket and honked his nose. A startled jay flew up out of the tree above us.

"Of course you do, Grampa. We all do." I felt my eyes start to sting and the back of my nose burned like I'd snorted up some cayenne pepper by mistake. My father had been gone over five years and the memory of him still felt raw sometimes, especially during sugaring season. I felt him hovering around us constantly as the sap began rising. I kept thinking I caught sight of him just beyond a distant tree and my heart would give a little lurch then a thud when my eyes adjusted to the woods and I knew they had been fooling me.

My mother said he was really there, visiting us in the

space between here and wherever there might be. She claimed to be on frequent speaking terms with him. The fact that he had been a man of very few words during his time on the mortal plane did little to strengthen my belief in her claims. It was all well and good to receive messages from the other side. He had given me a hand with advice on a number of occasions. Him visiting, that I could credit. It was his transformation into a chatterbox that beggared belief.

I patted Grampa's arm and waited quietly while he wrestled his emotions back under control. He missed his son and made no bones about it. We stood looking out over the woods and the sparkling snow, each of us thinking our own thoughts. After a bit Grampa blew his nose again with finality and tucked his handkerchief into his back pocket.

"So what brought you out here? I know it wasn't to hear me snuffling," Grampa said.

"A problem's come up with Russ and the basement at the town hall."

"Of course it has. I'm feeling pretty sore at whoever it was snagged Wesley for the general store project. Hopefully it will be done soon and he can give a hand to the restoration so we can really get moving," Grampa said.

"Wes isn't going to be able to help with this slowdown. There's no good way to say this. Russ found human remains in the basement under all the coal."

"You mean like a body?" Grampa stopped scanning the treetops for birds and gave me his full attention.

"A skeleton. Russ called me over to see it for myself before he called the police. He had cleared off what looked like a leg bone and part of a skull by the time I arrived. I'm not sure what Lowell and Mitch found after we left."

"You've had quite the morning, haven't you? Are you okay?"

"I'm fine."

"Do they have any idea who it could be?"

"Not that I know of. Lowell hustled us out of there pretty quickly after I called and there wasn't a wallet just lying there on the ground with a license in it or anything."

"What would a body be doing in the town hall under the coal? It must be thirty years since that space was used at all."

"And what were the spoons doing there?"

"Spoons?" Grampa leaned even closer.

"Russ found a pair of spoons near the leg bone. He didn't bother to tell Lowell but he blabbed about them at the Stack just as soon as he could cross the street."

"Did you see them?"

"I've got them right here. Russ left them on the counter in a hurry when Tansey fainted dead away when she saw them." I pulled the spoons from my jacket pocket and peeled away the napkin wrapper.

"Spooner Duffy." Grampa gave a long, low whistle and shook his head.

"What?" I had no idea what he could be talking about.

"I bet the body belonged to a guy named Spooner

Duffy. He always carried a pair of spoons in his pocket that looked just like those."

"Why would he do a thing like that?" There are some strange characters in Sugar Grove but I'd never heard of anyone with an overfondness for flatware. Unless you counted Marcella Petrie's light-fingered ways where other people's valuables were concerned.

"He played them. He played the spoons like people play other instruments. You should have heard him. Boy, was he some good!"

"How did he end up in the town hall basement? And why did Tansey take it so hard when she saw them?"

"Did she?" Grampa's usually open face shadowed over with an unusual guardedness.

"She did. Any idea why that would be? She is usually such a stoic woman. She swayed and keeled over right there in the Stack. From the looks of things she hit her head on the floor when she fell."

"Maybe she was in the throes of some sort of hormonal flux." Grampa blushed a bit right where his beard hair met the tops of his cheeks. He's not a prude per se but he isn't all that much for chatting about the workings of the human reproductive system in mixed company. Talking about bulls and heifers in the pasture was one thing. Mentioning a fellow Grange member's biology was quite another. I knew I must be on to something if my question had gotten him to offer up such an uncomfortable excuse.

"I'd say Tansey is a bit past such things. As a matter

of fact I've heard her say so with a great deal of relief. That can't be it."

"Maybe she is just overworked and exhausted. Knowlton is a good son but sometimes his taxidermical enthusiasms run away with him and he forgets his duties."

"Tansey thrives on hard work. When she runs out of things to do at her own place she runs all over town snatching items off other people's to-do lists just to feel justified in drawing breath each day."

"Perhaps it will just remain a mystery. Some things are best left that way, don't you think?" Grampa gave me a meaningful look. The sort of look that means the topic is dropped. Grampa is the kindest man I know. He is also the most stubborn. Once he's decided something is dropped, it's done. At least with him. I didn't need to agree with him. I just needed to take my questions elsewhere.

Fortunately, my mother never had any such looks to give. Closed topics conflicted with her core theories of proper child rearing.

I found her in the library breathing deeply and stretching her long arms over her head. Her peasant skirt was one she had tie-dyed herself back in the fall and the colors swirled and made me a little dizzy as she swayed back and forth in front of the spirituality section of the library shelving.

The library is a higgledy-piggledy assortment of classic works of literature, genre fiction, and reference books, which reflect the assorted specialty interests of the family. Most of the books in front of my mother were in what Celadon would call the "woo-woo" category. New Age religious works, the writings of famous Victorian Spiritualists, and guides to astral projection featured heavily on those shelves.

Celadon stuck to the gardening references, the history of architecture, and nutrition for growing children. That and a pile of bodice-ripping romances she never mentioned. She liked to pretend to be above such things but if you entered the room quietly enough you could catch her engrossed in a tatty paperback with a title written in raised gold letters. It did the heart good to clear your throat and watch her stuff the book under a cushion on the couch and pretend she was studying a painting on the wall instead.

Today, though, my mother and I were alone in the room with its bright shafts of sunlight streaming in and cheering things up. Even in winter it was a warm and friendly place to be and it was rare to find it unoccupied by at least one family member. I was glad. Mom might not think a topic was ever closed but she also could tell when other people weren't inclined to mention something. It was far better to get her on her own.

"Dani, how are the trees today?" She smiled at me.

"Nostalgic." I told her about Grampa and how vulnerable he was feeling then slid the topic round to where I wanted it. "Tansey's feeling a bit emotional, too."

"Tansey? That doesn't seem like her at all. Maybe I should run her natal chart and look for transits." Mom is always looking to the stars to explain the lives of those around her. She had each of our natal charts cast before she sent out birth announcements. I'm a Virgo. Don't get Celadon started on what that means in terms of my chances of marriage.

I told Mom about the call from Russ and the skeleton in the cellar. Then I told her about Tansey keeling over in the Stack.

"It seemed to be connected to the possibility that the body at the town hall was Spooner Duffy. Any idea why that would upset her so much?" There was usually no need to be subtle with my mother. Her mind wandered off in so many directions at the same time that her own thoughts obscured much of what others were saying to her anyway.

"Well, that doesn't make any sense at all. As far as I can remember, Tansey barely knew Spooner Duffy." Mom stopped swaying and gave me most of her attention. She still had a hazy look in her eyes like she was communing with the great beyond but she did turn to face me.

"Are you sure they weren't close? She took it really badly from the way it looked to me."

"Spooner was in town for only a few months and it was years ago. I guess I could be wrong about their level of connection."

"How long ago was he in town?"

"Well, let's see. Celadon was a toddler and I was

pregnant with Loden at the time. Spooner was at the baby shower. He played some spoons with the band at the shower. They were silver baby spoons, if I remember correctly. He said their tone was different than the ones he usually played." My mother's memory might be roundabout in nature but it was generally accurate about the things that mattered to her.

Baby showers definitely were on her list of favorite things to remember. I think that was one of the main reasons she was so sorry I hadn't produced any children yet. With two daughters she was expecting at least two more baby showers to be able to orchestrate. Nothing set her heart soaring like pretend cakes made out of cloth diapers.

"So almost thirty years, then?" I asked. I could see Mom doing the math in her head.

"That seems about right. It only seems like yesterday, though. Despite the fact Celadon's kids are older than she was then. Where does the time go?" With that Mom started sniffling just like Grampa had done out in the sugar bush. I was spreading goodness and light at a rate likely to outdo the Boy Scouts and the three local churches at the same time.

"But like you always say, Mom, time is just an illusion. Right now I'm sure there are an infinite number of dimensions with all of us at all different ages spread out across space and time." I reached up to pat her on the arm.

"Thanks, sweetie. I appreciate you trying to make me feel better. I know you don't believe that sort of thing any more than your father ever did." She tugged a lacy hankie out of the depths of her skirt pocket and dabbed at her eyes. "Of course, now he knows I was right but it isn't very nice to say 'I told you so' to someone who has passed through the golden gate." She turned back to the bookshelf and began swaying gently once more. I had all the information I was likely to get from her for now.

With so much to think about there was only one thing to do. I needed to work to get my mind off the morning and there was certainly plenty of work to be done at Greener Pastures during sugaring season. I filled a travel mug with coffee for the walk between the farmhouse and the sugarhouse. The sugarhouse is set a few hundred yards back from the main house and makes for a short but discernible commute.

There have been times, especially lately, when I wished my family life and my work life had a little more breathing room betwixt and between them but on a cold morning like this one I was glad to arrive at my destination without needing to scrape a car.

The woodstove was still smoldering away, keeping the place warm and the evaporator was chugging along doing its job of turning forty gallons of sap into a single gallon of syrup. There is a lot of excess water in the sap that needs to be boiled off. Educating the public about just what goes into making their syrup is one of the best parts of the job. Which is one of the reasons I love the maple festival so much. People come from all over the country and oftentimes the world to see for themselves how syrup is made and to participate in some winter fun.

The Greene family has been helping to organize and facilitate the festival for as long as it has been happening. Every year it gets a little bigger and in my opinion, a little better. Just the street food vendors alone are enough to make the drive worth it. There are maple-glazed doughnuts, maple bacon wrapped hot dogs, maple popcorn balls. Some vendors sell maple soda, others make crepes they drizzle with the sweet stuff.

Even though the festival is full of fun and worth every minute invested in its preparation, it does come at the busiest time of the year for the sugaring business. I wished every year there was a way to spread things out a bit more but there wasn't. The festival had to occur when things were in high gear in order to let the visitors see the inner workings of the maple industry.

One of the things we do through Greener Pastures is to educate people on the importance of land stewardship and the environmental impact of their daily decisions. People start to think more seriously about their choices when they understand that global warming may mean the end of the maple syrup industry. What we take for granted as a yearly occurrence may indeed end up obsolete.

I was adding a note to drop a dead man's spoons off at the police station to my yard-long to-do list when my cell phone rang with the tone I had assigned to Graham's number.

"I didn't see you at the Stack. Does that mean you got out of lunch with Hazel?"

"If only. She insisted we go to the coffee shop at Loon Lodge." Things were worse than I could have imagined. Loon Lodge was on the far side of Sugar Grove and it had a reputation as the place to go to rent a room on the cheap and on the sly.

"I am so sorry. Did you manage to stay put in the restaurant?" I hated to consider that my octogenarian aunt might have rounded more bases with Graham than I had managed to do myself. We had been seeing each other for a couple of months but they've been busy ones and I'm not a fast mover in the romance department even when my calendar is empty.

"It took some doing but I kept the both of us parked at a table in the center of the restaurant."

"How did you manage to avoid a dark booth in the back?"

"I shook my head at the waitress and flashed my badge. There was no way I was climbing into a booth with her. After the way she behaved in the truck on the way over I'd rather be mauled by a bear."

"She's got a bite like a pit bull. Once she sinks her teeth into someone almost nothing makes her let go."

"The only way I managed to steer her away from some deeply disturbing suggestions was to encourage her to talk about her granddaughter Jade."

"Good thinking. Jade is her Achilles' heel. How did you think to do that?"

"Fortunately, I read up on hostage negotiations in my spare time."

"How did you manage to escape?"

"I texted one of the other guys in the department and had him call me with an imaginary report of snowmobilers chasing a bull moose."

"Smart, but I bet she asked if she could ride along."

"She did. The only way I got out of it was to tell her she would have to surrender her flask while on duty."

"You really are a miracle worker."

"I just got lucky. I think it would be best if I didn't drop by until after Hazel finishes her visit." I felt my heart sink. I enjoyed it when Graham just popped in unexpectedly. The whole family seemed to love him. Which I guess was the problem. Some loved him too much.

"You're probably right. It may be awhile though. Hazel's visits tend to drag on."

"We'll just have to sneak around. It might be kind of fun."

"I've been thinking a lot lately about getting my own place. Maybe this is just the push I needed." As nice as living at home could be between the great food, even better company, and easy commute, there was the grandparents' overnight-guest policy to consider. They loved entertaining but if Graham stayed over he slept in the guest room. And there were questions about where I was going to be sleeping if I stayed out overnight.

"That sounds drastic."

"Drastic might be just what I need." I meant it, too. For some time I had been thinking it was time to push myself out of the nest. After all, how could I complain that the family treated me like a kid if I never lived like an adult?

We chatted a bit longer then disconnected and I fired up the computer and began scrolling through apartments-for-rent pages. I pulled out a pad of paper and halfheartedly made a note of several and the contact information. I was definitely interested in an apartment but I didn't want to move out of town.

All the places listed were at least fifteen minutes away when the roads were good. Here in New Hampshire that comprised about three months of the year. Between snow, frost heaves, potholes, and construction, which slowed things down for the other nine months, I'd be looking at a half-hour commute if I was lucky. Giving up on the Internet I started racking my brain for people I knew in town who might have a place to rent but no one came immediately to mind.

Five

I hadn't slept as well as usual. It seemed like half the night I dreamt about spoons rattling up against human bones. The other half I was holding the train of Hazel's wedding dress as she staggered down the aisle to meet her groom, Graham. What I needed more than anything was a walk in the sugar bush. Wandering among the trees always brightens my mood. Besides, during sugaring season the trees need checking every day.

I double-knotted my bootlaces, yanked my jacket zipper up to my chin, and pulled my hat down snug over my ears. Grandma knits up windproof hats from bulky wool so tight you can hold water in them. I was grateful for a new one in my Christmas stocking every year. Thus guarded against the elements I plunged out into the cold and stopped at the base of the sugarhouse porch long enough to strap on my snowshoes.

Crunching up along the trail to the woods I enjoyed the fresh air and the call of the blue jays announcing my arrival to all the other birds. Jay is the middle name of our police dispatcher, Myra. I wondered if it had turned her into the gossip she delighted in being.

My favorite birds, the chickadees, flitted here, there, and everywhere not even seeming to notice my appearance. I reached a tree with a plastic tube snaking round it and checked the line for flow. Everything seemed to be right as rain.

The month before the weather had been so cold the temperatures had never come close to above freezing. And that hadn't even taken windchill into account. The sun had been out every day for two weeks but the sap never budged a drop. It was simply too cold for anything to flow at all.

In order to make maple syrup you need cold nights and warm days. Now by warm I don't mean bathing suit weather, just temperatures a bit above freezing so the sap begins to run. Trees know when to wake up and I like to be there with a smile and a bucket when they do.

I had been out deep in the sugar bush for a couple hours checking taps and tubing when a twig snapped behind me. Knowlton was just standing there with his coat unzipped leaning up against a tree. He didn't look at me, which was unusual.

Generally Knowlton has to be beaten off with a stick studded with rusty nails and poisoned frog juice and even then he's hard to shake. But today, he didn't look like he even knew where he was. As much as I wanted to be the sort of person who could just keep going and leave him standing there all alone I couldn't.

"What's up, Knowlton? You're looking a little lost." I shocked myself even further by putting my hand on his sleeve. That managed to snap him out of his lethargy just a bit.

"Ma's not doing so good." So that was the trouble. All the girls in the Greene family interest Knowlton but no one replaces Tansey in his affections. Which may be why he is still available, but it is sort of sweet, too.

"Was she badly hurt in the fall?" It had been quite a distance from the counter stool to the floor and Tansey was not a young woman. The bruising alone had to be slowing her down.

"She's a bit stiff and there's a lump the size of a new potato on the back of her head but that's not the trouble."

"Well, what is?"

"You know how Ma always seems like she knows what she's doing even if she's got no reason to think so?" Knowlton asked. I nodded. Tansey was the sort who would think she could perform open-heart surgery on herself because she watched a twenty-minute video on the Internet. "She can't even decide what to have for breakfast. Yesterday she told me she was thinking about selling the farm and moving south."

"Moving south? Tansey overheats by mid-April. She must have hit her head harder than anyone thought. Did they do any scans at the hospital?"

"She wouldn't let them. Said it would cost too much."

"Why would she be talking about moving?"

"She won't say anything except that she wants me to have a good life. I told her I was staying here no matter what and she burst into tears."

"Tansey was crying?" This was more than I could imagine. Tansey didn't cry any more than she wore stockings and poufy dresses.

"At the breakfast table, right before she spooned some fried egg yolk into her coffee. I don't know what to do." Knowlton looked at me and his eyes were filling with tears. That was about enough of that. Work could wait.

"Come on. We're going to see your mother." I grabbed him by the arm.

"I can't go with you. She'll know I was talking about her and she will get even more upset."

"Fine. I'll go on without you. I'll tell her I'm stopping by on festival business. She won't know you spoke to me." Tansey was one of the co-chairs of the festival and it was necessary to speak to her from time to time. If she was unraveling about something it was going to impact the whole project.

"Thanks, Dani. Knowing you're gonna talk to her makes me feel even better than the news about Jade coming home to stay."

When I got back to the house I found Grandma in the kitchen peeling carrots into an enamelware pot we use for compostables. Her shoulders were pinned up around her ears the way they always were when stress made her gather in on herself. Hazel has that effect on a lot of people. Hazel was nowhere in sight but the evidence of her was already piling up. Enough shopping bags to fill a covered wagon completely cluttered the kitchen table.

Celadon was reaching a broom under the kitchen table in an effort to sweep up the dozens of glittery foil candy wrappers littering the floor. Despite the mess, the smell of freshly baked bread filled the air. Even though most nights Grandma fixed meals like she was running a logging camp this was a bit early in the day for her to get started. I had to wonder if she knew about Jade's visit even if Jade thought she had kept it a secret.

I sidled over to the pie safe and peeked through the door. Sure enough, a lemon meringue with the mile-high meringue sat on the middle shelf. Lemon meringue— Jade's favorite. On the top shelf there was a triple chocolate ecstasy cake, Celadon's preferred dessert.

I squatted down to check the bottom shelf. It was hard to tell what I was seeing through the screen. I pressed my nose closer and inhaled. That clinched it. Gingerbread. My favorite. Grandma definitely knew about Jade. And being the grandmother she was she didn't want to show favorites with desserts. Sure, she could have made Grampa's favorite, crème caramel with a maple sauce, but she didn't. She was trying to sweeten us all up and make us get along. We were in trouble.

"Grandma, are you expecting even more guests for dinner tonight?" I asked, shooting Celadon a loaded look behind our grandmother's back.

"What gives you that idea, my dear?" she asked. The

fact that she had not answered my question had not escaped my notice. Nor had the fact she kept her back turned toward me as she posed one of her own instead. Grandma doesn't make a habit of lying as far as I have ever noticed but she never seems to feel obligated to tell truths she deems hurtful or none of your business. I wasn't sure which she felt the news of Jade's arrival would be but I was sure it was one of the two.

"You only make more than one dessert on special occasions. You only make this combination of desserts on particularly memorable occasions." I pointed at the pie safe.

"Are you asking me a question?" This time, Grandma turned and gave me a firm stare. The stare that asked if I was sure I wanted to pursue my line of inquiry. It was the last chance she would give me before the gloves came off. Celadon saw it, too, and must have been in a charitable mood because she stepped up and took one for the team.

"What are you two talking about?" she asked.

"Knowlton says Jade is in town and that she's here to stay," I said. "She's the one who bought the general store and she's opening up a winery."

"A winery? If she wanted to run a winery, why not stick with the one her parents own in California?" Celadon made a good point. There were some wineries in New Hampshire but grapes aren't what the state is best known for. Staying where it was warmer should have made the most sense. Except for one thing.

"She's opening a sap wine winery. You know, wine

made from maple sap." We'd made it at Greener Pastures a few times ourselves on a small scale. It was light flavored and refreshing. As much as I hated to admit it, Jade might be onto something.

"How did you know she was here? And why didn't you tell us?" Celadon was going to be the grandmother staring her family down one day, that much was clear. I could see a flicker of pride chase a flash of annoyance across Grandma's face.

"It would behoove you girls to remember very little goes on in this town that I haven't heard about before most other people. That goes triple for things relating to my own family. Wesley Farnum knows when to keep his lips sealed and when to open them back up again. Jade's project was a small one. The jobs here at the farm just keep cropping up."

"And you didn't give us any warning?" Celadon's voice took on a plaintive note much like a peevish toddler. If I didn't know better I would have said we were still shorter than the countertop and being denied the chance to lick a batter bowl.

"Would it have made you happier to dread this day for the past few weeks? I think that I've done you both a favor."

"But where will she stay? We should have had time to prepare a place for her before she just descended on us." Celadon's voice tends to screech when she gets upset. My ears were starting to burn with the pitch of it.

"You make your cousin sound like a horde of locusts."

"She does tend to make a lot of noise and leave a path

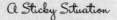

of devastation in her wake," I added, not wanting to leave Celadon all alone to take on Grandma. It was foolish of course, but the novel pleasure of siding with my sister was too alluring to resist.

"That's enough out of the pair of you. You haven't grown up a bit, either one of you, when it comes to Jade. She's family and we will treat her as such. As a matter of fact I want you to go into town right now and make her feel welcomed. Let her know I'm making her favorites for dinner." Grandma turned back to the carrots and left us to sort ourselves out. There was no court of higher appeal. Jade was here to stay and we would just have to lump it.

Six

We drove to town without speaking. I parked the minivan on the side of the road opposite the winery. I started to open the door to get out and get it over with when I felt Celadon clutch my arm.

"Would it be wrong to hide my daughter in the attic for the rest of her life and to tell Jade we sent her to boarding school?"

"It would be better to hide Spring at Piper's. Or maybe Tansey would let her move in. She needs cheering up."

"I'm not sure Tansey is a better influence than Jade. I mean, look how Knowlton turned out." Celadon had a point there. Knowlton still lived at home with Tansey and he spent his days stuffing roadkill and posing them in lifelike ways. His devotion to Celadon and myself verged on stalking. His worship of Jade crossed the line into religious ecstasy.

"Besides we'd miss her too much if she was away and then we'd run into Knowlton all the time when we visited."

"I'm just going to have to put my foot down and tell her Spring is not a life-size doll."

"That would be the mature thing to do." That did it. Reminding Celadon she was the mature one always moved her to action. She pried her fingers off my arm and stepped out onto the sidewalk. I followed her lead and headed for the shop.

I had to hand it to Jade—the girl had guts and big plans. Staring through the window, I realized I was impressed. I didn't want to be but I was anyway. The whole place just oozed of class and chic. From the gleaming patina on the wooden bar to the glint on the stainless steel barrels you felt like you were drowning in something a bit too good for real life. And there in the middle of it all was Jade, also a bit too good to be real.

Her hair was always just that little bit shinier, her eyes a bit brighter, her teeth naturally more even. She was five foot six in her stocking feet and you can bet there was a perfect pedicure hidden under those socks. She spun around to face the window as if feeling my stare and when she saw us, she waved a slim, tanned hand to beckon us in. My hand hadn't been darker than buttermilk since October.

I swallowed hard and looked over at Celadon. Her

jaw flexed and popped. She threw her shoulders back, reached out without looking for my arm, and dragged me along behind her as she pushed through the door.

"Now how could we throw a proper welcome if we had no idea you were coming?" Celadon said, making a beeline for Jade.

"And spoil the surprise? No way!" Jade leaned in and gave Celadon a peck on the cheek. "What do you think?"

"I think you managed to surprise us, all right." Celadon swiveled her head to take it all in. I could just hear the calculator tape whirling in her head as she totaled up the cost of the high-end materials and the ingredients for the product.

"Isn't it just beautiful?" Jade looked like she actually wanted to know what we thought. That was a first. As far as I could remember Jade had charted her own course and told others how they should chart theirs.

One of the most memorable examples of this was one summer when she advised my father to begin waxing his back if he wanted to be allowed to take her to the lake any longer. I seemed to remember her spending a lot of time alone at the house while the rest of us splashed and dove next to my furry father. But here she was ten years later setting up shop in a town full of men who would no more consider waxing their backs than they would flossing their teeth with a chainsaw.

I had to wonder what exactly had happened to either drive or tug her in our direction. After all, the closest high-end department store was more than thirty miles away and that was if you considered a place that sold tractors in addition to bras and washing machines high-end.

If you were in need of an establishment that carried socks that retailed for over twenty dollars per pair you were looking at a much longer hike than that. I asked myself if Jade had suffered from a traumatic brain injury. You know, the kind of thing that wiped out memory and even personality.

"It's got tons of eye appeal. It must have been a lot of work getting this set up. Especially since you did it long-distance," I said. Jade looked so eager for approval I couldn't just leave her dangling there. And what I said was true. The shop was beautiful. It looked just like the sort of thing she would design. In fact, even if I hadn't known she was responsible for it I would have had a queasy feeling in my gut that she was behind it all somehow.

"Thanks. It was a lot of work but it was tremendous fun, too. Now, I am hoping it will be even more fun to run. And I managed to get it up and running in time for the festival next month."

"I wanted to speak to you about the festival. Specifically the pageant." Celadon was starting to use the tone she always did with Mom when she wasn't about to listen to any more nonsense about astral projection or tarot cards.

"I won't have any time to worry about the pageant this year. I'll be much too busy running my business."

"So you are planning to stay and operate it yourself?"

Celadon asked. I heard her jaw pop again and the temperature in the room dropped by a few degrees. I could almost see Celadon's breath in the air as the words left her lips.

"I am. It was time for a change and I knew exactly what I wanted to turn my hand to next. I've always had a soft spot for Sugar Grove and with all the free sap from the family trees I'm bound to make a go of it." Jade turned one of her high-wattage smiles full force on me. I was trying to keep my own smile from slipping off my face but I could feel it moving southward like drips from an ice cream cone on a sunny August afternoon.

"Free sap from the family trees? Have you talked this over with Grampa or Grandma?" I asked.

"What's there to talk about?" Jade shook her head at me and rolled her eyes.

"Congratulations on all your hard work. Will you be coming by the house for dinner? Our grandmother's making all your favorites," Celadon asked as she dug her fingers into my elbow in her preferred way of letting me know I should be quiet.

"Well, of course I will. Hazel's picking me up at closing time and bringing me and some of my stuff over."

"What kind of stuff?" I asked, hoping I hadn't a clue.

"Clothing, makeup, personal possessions." Jade rolled her eyes again. "You know, the stuff you keep in the place where you live."

"So you're intending to live at Greener Pastures?" I asked.

"Where else would I live?"

"And where do you expect to be sleeping?" I asked but I was pretty sure the answer would be the same as it had been for all the years we were growing up.

"Your room, of course." Jade rolled her eyes again. "Or should I say our room."

"Since you're planning to be here awhile you might want to get Doc MacIntyre to take a look at your eyeballs. They seem to be rattling round loose in your head." With that Celadon dragged me back out of the store and halfway down the block before releasing my elbow.

"I don't know about you but I can't go home yet," Celadon said. "I know I'll say something I'll regret, most likely to Grandma. And it isn't like this is her fault."

"You need a distraction."

"Usually I'd stop in at the opera house and check on the work but with progress being held up by the body in the cellar I am at loose ends."

"Why don't I drop you off at the town hall anyway for a couple of hours? You can make a call to Wesley Farnum. The only good news this morning was that since he's done at Jade's he might be available to work on the restoration project. When you're done with that you could head over to the library."

"Where are you going?"

"I promised Knowlton I would look in on Tansey since he says she isn't doing too well after her fall. But I need to stop in at the doc's place first. I want to find

59

out if Tansey'll be up for some visitors or if I should wait awhile. Did you want to go to Doc's, too?"

"Certainly not. I couldn't possibly take Jade and Yahtzee all in one morning." We drove a couple of blocks to the town hall and Celadon hopped out.

"I'll pick you up in a couple of hours." I waved and drove off toward the puzzle shop for a bribe for the doctor.

Doc MacIntyre's house sat two streets back from the main road through town. The location was convenient for him and for the patients who had reason to visit his office. The doc made a lot of house calls, too. With no public transportation system in Sugar Grove, or much of the state, truth be told, he often tended to the elderly in their own homes.

I slid the Midget into a spot at the far side of the parking area and checked my purse for the pad of Yahtzee score sheets I knew I'd need to offer to have a chance of loosening the doctor's lips. Every man has a price. Some will sell their souls for booze and some for the promises of affection from a pretty young woman. For others, their sweet tooth leads them around like a pig with a nose ring.

For the doc it was his unquenchable desire to play Yahtzee. It was never a good idea to show up healthy, or even just a little bit sick at the doctor's office without urgent business that needed you elsewhere or you'd better be prepared to play a few rounds.

I pushed open the hot pink door of his office and almost tripped over his big tomcat, Brutus. People with a cat allergy usually choose to go to the doctor in the next town over because Brutus is always in the office, sometimes even in the exam room, depending on how much he likes the patient. Brutus isn't too particular. He likes most people. We've always gotten along just fine. For which I am grateful, considering his size.

Brutus is not a cat you'd be wise to offend. He's twenty-five pounds of fluff-covered muscle. Once he got fleas so bad the doctor had him shaved. With all his fur gone he looked like a competitive bodybuilder on one of the sports channels whenever he walked around the room.

I bent down to give him a pat, then listened for the doctor's booming voice from inside his exam room. Upon hearing it I took a seat in the tiny waiting room and picked up a ragged copy of *Reader's Digest*. Before I had finished increasing my word power Doc yanked open the exam room door and ushered William Foley out through it.

Will scowled at me but I didn't take it to heart. His face is just one of those permanently set in a scowl and he doesn't mean anything by it. I've seen his wedding photos. He scowled at his bride, Eunice, through all of them. They've been married fifty-four years and according to Eunice, he's never said a cross word to her in all that time.

"You let me know if that ointment doesn't work, now, you hear?" Doc said, thumping William gently on the shoulder. William scowled at him, dipped his head at me in greeting, then shuffled out the door.

"Dani, what brings you by? You haven't come down with something just as sugaring season is starting up, have you?" The doctor's voice was completely oversize for the tiny space. If he didn't lower his volume I was going to have an earache. Or become spontaneously deaf.

"No, no. Nothing like that. I was actually wondering if you've spoken to Tansey."

"About what?"

"Well, she was so upset about Spooner Duffy's body being found in the town hall I thought she might have ended up needing to see you."

"Well, even if she did there is no way I could tell you about it. My patient visits are confidential."

"I didn't want to pry into her business. I was just worried about her. It isn't like Tansey at all to be so upset about anything. She's always such an even-tempered person."

"Not much fazes her, I will say that."

"I didn't want to go over to her house with a Bundt ring and check on her without having a better idea of her mind-set. I wouldn't want to upset her even further." I drew the pad of Yahtzee score sheets out of my purse and fanned through them. "I was sort of hoping you might put my mind at ease over a quick game. But, if that would violate your sense of medical ethics I understand." I moved the pad back to the opening of my bag.

"Now I didn't say I couldn't give you any perspective concerning Spooner. He wasn't here long enough to ever be a patient of mine but he sure did leave an impression on the town."

"That surprises me. No one seems to remember much

about him." I followed Doc as he left the office and headed for his small, bright kitchen. The woodstove was fired up red-hot and a pot of coffee sent out a delicious smell into the room.

"People remember all right. They just wish they didn't. You pour us a couple of cups of coffee and I'll grab the Yahtzee." He returned before I'd poured half of the first cup, a warm glow on his face and his battered game box clutched to his chest.

"So why would they want to forget a guy who wasn't even in town long enough to get sick? And how could he have ended up in the basement?"

"Spooner's real name was Garland. He hitchhiked into town one late fall day with nothing but a backpack on his back and a pair of spoons in his pocket. He stopped in at the Stack Shack and told Glenda and Willis he was looking to do some odd jobs. He liked the look of Sugar Grove, he said, and wanted to stay a little while and needed to make some money."

"Sounds like a pretty normal thing to have happen. People are always falling in love with Sugar Grove on sight."

"That's exactly how it was. Glenda pointed to the notice board in the back of the Stack and told him to try there for something. When he said nothing seemed like it was a good fit she recommended he talk to Tansey."

"So Tansey did know him, then?"

"She did indeed. Spooner waited around all morning for Tansey to come in for lunch. When she did he walked right over and told her he was the right man for the job."

"What job was that?" I asked.

"That's what Tansey asked, too. He laughed and said any job she might need doing. He'd heard she was a tough woman with a hardscrabble farm and he had a skillful and willing pair of hands if she would give him room, board, and a few bucks at the end of the week."

"That's pretty enterprising of him."

"It sure was. Tansey may have been impressed at his gumption but she wasn't no different in those days than she is now. She told him she was doing fine on her own and that she didn't need any help from any strange men."

"Then what happened?"

"Spooner gave her a little bow, thanked her for her time, and headed out the door."

"That's it?" I was expecting much more somehow.

"Of course it isn't. Tansey had a bunch of errands to run in town that afternoon and it wasn't until close to suppertime that she got back home to her place. When she pulled up the lights were on in her house."

"Was she scared?"

"Tansey wouldn't be scared of a *T. rex* running at her with a knife and fork clutched in its claws. No, she just pulled the shotgun out from behind the seat of her pickup truck and made sure it was loaded before hustling into her kitchen."

"Was anyone there?"

"Spooner was there. He had a tea towel tied around his waist like an apron and he was bent over the stove, poking at some trout he was frying."

"What did Tansey do?"

"What could she do? She hired him. Not only had he caught the fish for supper and cooked them, he had split and stacked a cord of wood, changed the washer in the leaking kitchen faucet, and recaulked her tub. He even dusted and vacuumed."

"That still doesn't explain how he came to be in the cellar of the town hall."

"No, it doesn't."

"Or why no one wants to talk about him. He sounds like he was a great guy."

"I haven't gotten to that part yet. Spooner was real popular in town, especially with the ladies. He didn't just carry spoons in his pocket for no reason. He played them. He was a regular feature at the music nights over in the opera house. Everyone loved to hear what he could do with those things. The novelty of it was just something else, I tell you."

"I bet. So what happened to change public opinion?"

"The library."

"The library got him ostracized?"

"Well, the fund-raising for the library. You know how the profits from the Sugar Grove Maple Festival go to a worthy project in town each year?"

"Of course." For generations the people of Sugar Grove have raised money for one cause or another through their festival. The town opens its arms to tourists from all over and finds a lot of ways to entertain them. The festival has paid for an ambulance, an after-school program, and the local food pantry. This still didn't explain the problem of Spooner becoming persona non grata.

"Monday morning after the festival was over the town clerk found the lock jimmied and all the money they raised over the weekend missing. No one ever saw Spooner again."

"So everyone assumed he was the one who took the money?"

"They didn't want to think so but it did look that way. The money was never recovered and when Lowell questioned Tansey about it she said he never came home that night."

"Well that doesn't look too good, does it?" I felt sorry for Tansey. And curious, too. I wondered how close they were and how bad she must have felt by the betrayal. I know it would have really hurt me.

"It won't look good if a bunch of money is found with his body either."

"Even if it is, he never made it out of town. He never used any of the money. How did he end up murdered in the basement if he was running off with the funds?" I asked.

"We won't know that he was murdered until the results come back from the lab. He may have fallen and hit his head on something."

"No. I saw the body. He was on his back and he had been buried," I said.

"So you think someone else was responsible for his death?"

"I do. A dead man doesn't bury himself. Who was here and likely to have had a problem with him back then?" I asked.

"No one that I can think of. Like I said, he was well liked by most of the ladies."

"And it has been thirty years since it happened. Maybe you forgot something you used to know." I hated to even mention it but sometimes the doctor got slightly duffer-headed.

"I suppose it could be possible. So many things have happened over the years some things might have slipped through the cracks. But nothing stands out. Other than the money being gone along with Spooner."

"Tansey must have been pretty upset to have thought she was sheltering a felon all that time in her home."

"She was completely silent on the whole matter, that much I do remember. It was like he had never existed."

"That seems extreme. A lot of people would have wanted to vent their anger."

"Not Tansey. She was as silent as the grave. Maybe more so."

"So why do you think she got so upset when his body was found? Was it a delayed reaction, do you think?"

"That certainly would be considered delayed. Thirty years is more than your lifetime." More than a lot of people's. Which got me thinking. If I wanted some answers I ought to go straight to the source:

Seven

I pulled up at Tansey's feeling in over my head. Tansey and I have a relationship complicated by competing agendas. It's her top priority to marry me off to Knowlton and it is mine to thwart her efforts. We're cordial, cooperative even, when the task at hand suits us both the same way but the rift about Knowlton is always there in the center.

I try to step round it whenever possible but Tansey wades in up to her neck and then shakes the topic all over me like a dog fresh from a bath. I promised Knowlton I'd help and I was concerned for Tansey's welfare but this meddling could be perceived as something different than I intended. I took a deep breath to calm my nerves and headed for the sugarhouse end of Tansey's barn.

"Dani, what are you doing here? I'd've thought you'd

be up to your eyeballs in sap right about now." Tansey sat slumped in a tatty aluminum folding chair with frayed webbing. Her feet sprawled out in front of her and she hadn't bothered to tie her boots.

"And I'd have thought you'd be busy, too. Is your evaporator broken down or something?" Tansey's sugar-house looked like it was the off-season. Her evaporator was empty, no fire heated the box. Tansey herself wasn't labeling jugs while she sat in her chair. In fact, there were no jugs to be seen and Tansey, for the first time since I'd known her, was doing absolutely nothing.

"I'm not sure I'm gonna boil any sap this year." She glared at me, her chin tilted up at me like she was daring me to chide her. When I looked closely I could tell she was biting the inside of her cheek. It was a technique I used when I was a kid and was trying not to cry.

Even though this was new territory for us I didn't feel good about turning tail and leaving her with her thoughts. She looked like she could use a friend. The best thing to do for Tansey would be to just get straight on with it. She didn't respect people who dithered. They annoyed her.

"What has your sugaring got to do with Spooner Duffy?" I asked as I lowered myself gently into the chair next to hers. It gave a wrenching squeaking sound but I still heard her gasp over the ruckus of the twisting metal.

"Spooner Duffy? Who's that?" Tansey bit back down on her cheek. If we didn't hurry up this conversation she was going to need stitches.

"The odd-jobs guy who lived here and helped out with things about thirty years ago. The guy whose spoons knocked you for a loop. That Spooner Duffy."

"Oh. Him."

"I'm not trying to be nosy. I'm worried about the festival. People are counting on you to help organize things. Without you the whole thing will most likely fall apart." I wasn't just flattering her. Tansey was one of the few people in town who knew just about everything there was to know about the festival. If she was out of commission, my life and the lives of all my family members was about to get a lot less enjoyable. And there was already enough of that going around with Hazel and Jade in town.

"Oh, don't worry. I'll hold up my end of any festival business." Tansey tried to sit up a little straighter but just sagged back against the chair webbing.

I hadn't seen that kind of exhaustion in someone since my father died. My grandparents and my mother had looked exactly that same way. I probably had, too, but I really wasn't in the habit of looking at myself in the mirror all that often.

"I've seen that look before, Tansey. You loved that guy and now you know he's dead and likely has been for a good long time. It's a terrible thing to find out and even worse when the news is delivered so tactlessly." I watched as Tansey slumped even deeper into her chair. "I remember getting the news about my father. I'd just gotten back a paper I had worked really hard on. I remember I was still standing outside the classroom door staring at the A on the top of it, just swelled up with pride and relief when my cell phone rang. It was Lowell calling to tell me my father had died. My legs went out from under me and I dropped to the floor. I wasn't expecting anything like that."

"No, of course you weren't. It was just a normal day and then it all fell apart." Tansey leaned forward and patted my knee with her callused hand.

"That's it exactly. One second you are going about your regular business and the next you've become unmoored. It's a terrible thing to find yourself without a father." I had really meant to be a comfort to Tansey but I felt a lump tightening in my throat.

I looked up and thought I had made things even worse because a tear was sliding down Tansey's weather-beaten cheek. I never thought I'd see the day Tansey Pringle cried. The world must be tilting on its axis. Before I had a chance to say something comforting she spoke.

"It is a terrible thing to be without a father. My Knowlton has lived with that particular disadvantage all his life. I thought it was for the best that he not know anything about his father but now I'm not so sure."

"What does this have to do with Knowlton?" A light was starting to dawn but I thought it best if I let her share the news instead of me grabbing at it.

"Spooner was Knowlton's father."

"And you decided not to tell anyone because everyone thought Spooner ran off with the money from the festival?"

"That's right. It may be difficult to understand now but when I was pregnant with Knowlton the world was still hard on unwed mothers. It was gonna be tough enough on my baby to be raised up without a father but for everyone to say his daddy was a thief, too, was not something I was prepared to saddle him with."

"Did you love him?"

"Lord, help me, I did. I loved that man like I didn't know I could love anyone. When he up and left me my heart just went dead. Until I held our baby in my arms for the first time. I've spent thirty years giving all that love to Knowlton, trying to make up for his missing father. Hoping if I loved our boy well enough Spooner might feel it somehow and find his way back to us." Tansey dragged a flannel-clad arm across her eyes. I was completely stunned. She had always seemed obsessed with Knowlton but now it all made sense.

"At least you know why he never made it back to you."

"That's something, I guess. But now the past is all dredged up again and I am worried everyone is going to know about Knowlton being Spooner's son."

"Would that be a problem if Spooner didn't steal the money?"

"No. I can't say it would. Now that's an idea." Tansey struggled up to the edge of the chair, a hopeful flicker in her eyes. I didn't like the look of it any more than I had liked the way she had seemed so depressed. I liked Tansey best when she was her normal no-nonsense self. But I had to ask.

"What is?"

"You could poke around and ask a few questions about the investigation."

"Why me?"

"Because you're the police chief's goddaughter. And, if it wasn't for your renovation project Spooner would never have been found. You owe this to Knowlton."

"How do you figure that?" I didn't like to think of owing Knowlton anything. Just the idea of him having a hold over me made my skin crawl like I'd had accidentally taken an overdose of antihistamines.

"People are bound to talk and they may put two and two together about me and Spooner. If your project hadn't unearthed him none of that would have happened. You've got to help clear Spooner's name before Knowlton is connected with him." Tansey stood up out of her chair like our business was concluded. I took my cue from her and followed her to the door.

"But what if I can't? I'm not an investigator and I'm out straight between the sugaring and the festival."

"You're a born snoop, and I mean that in a good way. And if you don't help me with this your schedule is about to get a lot busier because I won't be able to show my face in town. And that means I won't be able to help with the festival. You'll be on your own."

Eight

 "Yup, the chief's in. You got something special on your mind?" Myra asked, as eager as ever for something juicy to share at the Stack come lunchtime.

"Can't a girl just want to stop in and say hello to her favorite godfather?" I pushed on past her desk and poked my head around Lowell's office door. His back was to me and he had his chair tipped back, his fingers laced behind his head. I cleared my throat and smiled at him when he turned around.

"How's your grandmother holding up with Hazel in the house?" Lowell asked.

"She's spending a lot of time in the laundry room starching and ironing the sheets," I said as I stepped in and closed the door behind me.

"That bad?"

"Hazel believes laundry is beneath her. Even though

she grew up in the house I'm not sure she even knows where the laundry room is located."

"Your grandmother is a smart cookie. But she's not why you are here, is she?"

"Have you identified the body yet?"

"There hasn't been much to go on."

"Maybe this will help." I pulled the napkin-wrapped spoons from my jacket pocket and placed them on the desk.

"What's this?" Lowell reached out and unwrapped the small bundle.

"Something Russ found with the body."

"Why didn't he give it to me at the town hall?"

"He said he forgot he had it but I think he wanted to have a souvenir of his big adventure. You know, something to brag about to his wife and kids."

"How'd you get it?"

"He headed to the Stack right after he left the town hall and was showing these off to Tansey and Piper. Tansey fainted dead away when she saw them."

"Myra let me know Tansey had some sort of fit but no one said what brought it on. So Russ just left them there?"

"He left the restaurant in an awful hurry without them when he saw the effect they had on Tansey."

"You should have turned these in right away."

"I thought about it. I came by to turn them in but you weren't here and I didn't want to give Myra anything else to gossip about."

"I guess I can see your point."

"I think I know who they belonged to, too. Do you

remember a guy named Spooner Duffy?" I asked, watching Lowell's eyes widen as he heard the name.

"Of course I do. There was a lot of flap when he and the fund-raiser money went missing at the same time."

"Tansey and Grampa both identified these spoons as belonging to him."

"Well that would explain how he never could be tracked down after the money disappeared."

"So someone went looking for him years ago?"

"Everyone thought he made off with a whole lot of money. We certainly did go looking for him."

"How much money are we talking about?" I was curious how much the fund-raiser made before I was born.

"All told, about twelve thousand dollars. Which would be somewhere around thirty thousand dollars now."

"Did you work on the case?"

"Both the chief and I worked it for months. I've got the file on it right here somewhere." Lowell spun in his chair to face a beat-up metal file cabinet. He yanked open a drawer and tugged out a file. "The chief was always sore that we never closed this one."

"And you never found the money either?"

"No we didn't. Not a trace of it."

"How did you hear about the theft?"

"Here it is, March 26, 1984. We got a call from Karen Brewer. She was the town clerk at the time and when she got to work on Monday morning Jim Parnell was already standing at the door waiting for her."

"What did Jim have to do with any of this?"

"When he was just starting out in the real estate

business he was always on the lookout for ways to get his name out in the community. He was one of the heads of the festival committee. He'd left the money in a bank deposit bag in Karen's locked desk drawer in her office at the town hall. He was there to pick it up and to run it to the bank to deposit it."

"But it wasn't there?"

"No. The desk lock had been picked and the bank bag was empty. Karen called us in immediately."

"Did someone force their way into the town hall, too?"

"Well that was part of the problem. The locks on the outside doors to the town hall hadn't been forced, at least not that we could see. It looked like someone had used a key." Which didn't necessarily mean that narrowed down the list of suspects by very much. Lots of people had keys to lots of places in Sugar Grove, like the Grange hall or the churches.

"Why was Spooner suspected? Was it just because he left at the same time as the money disappeared?"

"It was that and the fact that he was one of the people with a key. The selectmen hired him to paint the inside of the town hall and it was easier for him to do the work when the town hall was closed."

"So it looked like he took it?"

"He was the primary suspect. According to Tansey, after the festival finished up on Sunday night he was planning to do some more work on the town hall job. No one ever saw Spooner again after Sunday evening."

Nine

I returned from my errand at the police station and spent what little was left of the day working in the sugarhouse. Before I knew it the sky was dark and Celadon's voice was crackling through the intercom we have connecting the main house to the sugarhouse.

"Grandma says supper is on the table and all Greene backsides are to be in their seats in the dining room in two minutes. You know how Grampa is about cold food."

For such an easygoing guy Grampa is rabid about the temperature of his food. The only time I've heard him raise his voice to any of us was when Loden came in fifteen minutes after we were called to the table. A skin puckered the surface of the gravy in its boat as Grampa poured it onto his mashed potatoes. Suffice it to say none of us was ever late again. Loden still doesn't like gravy.

I hurried back to the house as fast as my dread-filled legs could manage. Jade was sure to be at the table, sitting right where she always did. The light from the chandelier would hit her hair in just such a way as to make her look like an angel in a shampoo commercial. She'd compliment the cook and get away with not washing the dishes afterward. Just thinking about all of it made me lose my appetite.

Until I got to the table. Grandma had outdone herself. Sure I was miffed about Jade's arrival and how Grandma had kept that information to herself but it is hard to hold a grudge when you are looking at one of my grandmother's hams. Grampa sat at the head of the table with a fork and knife in his hands, ready to carve. Everyone was in their seat. Except for Hazel and Jade.

Supper at Greener Pastures is always at six o'clock. Always. Grampa doesn't like to eat so early as to still have any lunch taking up room in his belly. He wants the whole business cleared out and ready for more of whatever my grandmother might decide to magic onto the table. By having a set suppertime he is sure to be prepared.

And prepared he was. His fists clenched and tensed on the worn wooden handles of the carving set with the same rhythmic talent Celadon had displayed when she had been popping her jaw earlier. As much as Grampa adored his older sister I wouldn't want to be either Hazel or Jade whenever they decided to arrive.

Grampa checked his watch. Everyone else shifted silently in his or her seats. The smell of the ham filled the dining room. My mouth was so full of water from the delicious aromas I wished I had one of those suction straws like they use at the dentist's office. Not only was there a ham, Grandma had baked fresh rolls, made her famous carrot and turnip mash and au gratin potatoes with just a hint of nutmeg.

At six twenty Grampa cleared his throat. "Looks like we might as well get started. This all looks delicious, my love." He tried to wink at Grandma but didn't quite manage to pull it off. Everyone rushed to talk all at once to fill the quiet. No sense ruining one of Grandma's meals on account of the rudeness of others. At least not as far as I could see.

Even though the food was outstanding it was hard to enjoy it to full capacity. Grandma tried to hide her disappointment under idle prattle but her face looked stricken. You could tell Grampa was upset by the way he was off his feed. He ate only three helpings of ham and four of the potatoes.

For a man who requires his own butter dish at dinner each evening this was saying a lot. Grandma's au gratin potatoes are one of his favorite things. He's mentioned he wants to be buried with a recipe card for them tucked into his shirt pocket right next to his heart.

"Should we call Lowell?" Loden finally asked. I imagined his question echoed everyone else's thoughts. No one had ever completely missed one of Grandma's meals unless they had been unconscious at the time. For example, my father had been late for dinner once when I was six. His truck had slid off an icy road with a hairpin curve and had tumbled nose-first into a ravine. Fortunately, he was wearing a seat belt but he still ended up cracking three ribs and knocking himself unconscious.

I hoped for their sakes Hazel and Jade were at least as injured. Besides, if they were seriously hurt Jade could stay at the hospital until I found an apartment instead of bunking in my room with me.

"Lowell says they'll be along any minute. No one needs to worry." My mother decided to chime in with something that from the expression on her face meant she was trying to be helpful. Grandma didn't seem inclined to agree. Grandma's face puckered up like a drawstring bag getting a good solid yank from a person with a beefy hand.

"I don't think that means no one should worry," Celadon said. She tapped her fork against the edge of her plate the way she always did when a lesser woman would start swearing a blue streak.

"They will do as they're a mind to. And so shall we. Who wants dessert?" Grandma asked, a plastic smile fixed on her face.

Despite the quality of all three desserts the meal ended on a dismal note. Loden ate only one piece of each offering and Celadon took just a sliver of the triple ecstasy cake and looked like it pained her to choke it down.

By the time the table was cleared and I had my arms sunk up to the elbows in hot steamy soapy water I was glad to be alone instead of struggling to pretend every-thing was fine. The back door into the kitchen popped open before I had finished scrubbing the pots. Lowell, Hazel, and Jade all trooped in, dragging a trail of mud.

"I thought you said you'd be here for dinner," I said to them. Jade stomped past me with an overnight bag slung over her shoulder. I heard the sound of her boots clattering up the stairs.

"We were unavoidably delayed," Hazel said. Her fedora sat askew on her head and she was limping. Which I assumed was on account of her injudicious choice in footwear. No sensible woman runs out on errands when the snow is knee-deep in a pair of leopard-print pumps with three-inch heels. Especially women in their eighties.

"You're not hurt, are you?" The thought of having to provide Hazel with any sort of nursing care flash-froze my very marrow.

"Of course not," she said. On closer inspection I could see her awkward gait was caused by the lack of a heel on her left shoe. "No thanks to that car of yours." She shed both shoes and hurried after her granddaughter.

"What did she mean, *No thanks to my car*?" My MG Midget was my prized possession. It had belonged to my father, who had restored it when I was a kid. After he died I had taken to driving it myself. In the past few months it had survived a cassowary attack and a run-in with a key-wielding vandal. It had been in the body shop more often than out of it lately.

I'd been driving the family minivan most of the time

recently in order to save wear and tear. Between the potholes and the frost heaves and the fact that I was on the outs with my mechanic I hadn't wanted to risk anything happening to it.

"There's been an incident." Lowell pointed to a chair at the kitchen table. "I think you should sit." Lowell isn't inclined toward unnecessary drama. I sat.

"Does Hazel need a lawyer? Loden's around here somewhere." My older brother practiced law but only under duress. Even though he was a member in good standing of the New Hampshire bar he preferred making additions to his model train set instead and only provided legal counsel to townspeople who couldn't otherwise afford the help he was willing to provide free of charge.

"Fortunately, no. The young man she had with her during the accident wasn't underage."

"What kind of an accident?"

"She decided to drive the Midget over to pick up Jade. According to the kid the rescue crew pulled out of the passenger seat, she endeavored to have a little fun first." Images of tangled steel and torn upholstery flashed through my mind. Hazel's ideas of fun generally could not be described in terms of good or clean. Lowell was not the first policeman to have brought her home.

"She picked up a boy and took him joyriding in my car?"

"That's the gist of it. He says he was leaving the Gulp and Go. Before he knew what happened Hazel had sweet-talked him into the seat beside her and was flying down the road like she was piloting a magic carpet.

They were catching air like the little car was a kite." Lowell shook his head. I'm not sure if it was disbelief or admiration. Hazel has that effect on a lot of people, especially men.

"He must have had one heck of a sweet tooth to let a little old lady convince him to get into the car with her."

"I expect she singled him out because of it. He said he was just standing there with a hot chocolate in one hand and a candy bar in the other when she pulled up next to him and revved the engine."

"What about my car?"

"I'm not sure. When I left, Byron had just gotten there with the tow truck. What I do know was the rescue guys had to use the jaws of life on the door to get the kid out."

"The kid wasn't hurt, was he?"

"No, just thoroughly rattled. I don't expect he'll be taking rides with strange ladies again any time soon."

"It sounds like my car might not be in the position to be driven soon either." I was so angry at Hazel my head felt light and my skin was prickling with heat. And knowing Hazel, she wouldn't even consider apologizing let alone offering to arrange for the repairs.

"I can't say for sure. What I can tell you is Byron just took one look at it and shook his head. He didn't have anything to say at all." The news about my car was bad. The fact that Byron had been the one to tow it off made it awkward as well. Byron had been the only one I had trusted to work on my car since my father died but a few weeks earlier we had exchanged some heated words and hadn't spoken since.

I knew apologizing was the right thing to do but I had managed to repeatedly convince myself I was too busy. I felt like the universe was kicking me in the pants and reminding me to act like a civilized adult. I hate it when that happens.

"This situation calls for dessert. You want something? Grandma made three kinds on account of Jade's homecoming."

"Is lemon meringue one of them?"

"Of course."

"Sold." Lowell leaned back in his chair and his eyes drooped a bit at the corners.

"How's your investigation going?" I asked, placing a wide wedge of pie in front of him. I settled into a chair opposite with a square of gingerbread dolloped with whipped cream. It wouldn't have been polite to leave him to eat alone.

"Even with the body identified there hasn't been much progress. I'm starting to think there may never be any." I thought about Tansey's request and the possible line of inquiry it might open if Lowell were aware of her relationship with Spooner.

"There's something I didn't tell you the other day about Spooner." Lowell's hand paused halfway to his mouth.

"Which was?"

"Tansey asked me to try to prove Spooner didn't steal the money."

"And why would she do that?"

"Spooner was Knowlton's father. Tansey's afraid your

investigation is going to drag everything up and make things difficult for Knowlton."

"There were rumors at the time about Tansey and Spooner. I don't think Tansey ought to worry."

"Well she is worried. I'd say worried sick. She won't leave her house, and is considering selling up and moving south."

"Why does she think you should help instead of the police?" Now I was embarrassed. Being called a snoop had not been flattering at the time and I had no desire to repeat what she had said.

"She values my discretion and suggested that my nonprofessional status would stir up less curiosity than questions from the authorities." I felt my posture improving and my lips starting to pucker primly. Every time I lie I turn into a Victorian spinster version of myself.

"Judging by the way you look like you're sucking on a pickled egg I'm going to guess that what she really said was you're an effective snoop."

"Something like that."

"I'm sure she meant it kindly enough." Lowell took a big bite of pie. It was hard to feel irritated when he was right and when he had bits of fluffy meringue clinging to his mustache.

"That's exactly what she said. It was sort of embarrassing but she really felt I could help. You're not going to tell me to butt out, are you? Tansey threatened to drop out of helping with the festival if I didn't do something to clear Spooner's name."

"I'll tell you what. I don't mind if you poke around

asking some questions about Spooner and what people have to say about the missing money as long as you tell me what you discover."

"Thanks. You're the best." I reached over with a napkin and dabbed at Lowell's mustache.

"You might want to have a cover story for your questions. Have you thought of one?"

"Telling them I'm working on a commemorative booklet to celebrate the fiftieth year of the festival might work."

"Sounds perfect. Just remember, this doesn't make you a police detective. Stay out of trouble and if you're getting any sense someone is especially riled up you get ahold of me immediately. Okay?"

"Got it. Any idea where I should start?"

"Why don't you go talk to Karen Brewer, the former town clerk? After all, the money went missing from inside her desk drawer at the town hall. And maybe some of the people who were questioned at the time. Like Jim Parnell and Cliff Thompson. Maybe they'll be willing to share more now than when the incident happened in the first place."

Ten

Grampa, Loden, and I were up at the crack of dawn checking on the trees and the lines and the status of the evaporator. I may have agreed to help Tansey but the sap wasn't about to wait while I ran around asking people thirty-year-old questions. Sap can go bad if not properly handled, just like any other food product. If too much time elapses between collecting it and boiling it down it spoils and has to be thrown out.

I can't think of too many things that feel more wasteful to me than that. We try our best not to waste a drop. With so much sap needed to produce a single gallon of finished syrup we don't have a drop to waste.

As I hustled through the woods I thought of Mindy Collins and her new sugaring business. Even with all the help from the family, sugaring is a big job requiring a lot of effort, made easier by so many willing hands and by using modern practices.

Mindy's husband, Russ, might not be working on the opera house because of the investigation but I'd be willing to bet the chance for an early spring that he wasn't pitching in with the syrup making at their place instead. I was even more grateful than usual for my family and the feeling of teamwork sugaring season always brought out in us.

Most of us, that is. The night before when I had finished talking with Lowell I dragged myself up to my room where I was not surprised in the least to see Jade flung across the spare bed, the contents of her overnight bag spread across everything else. I had to remove the bag itself from my own bed in order to crawl under the covers. Jade had not been in a talkative mood and had kept her eyes squeezed shut when my alarm went off well before the birds were chirping.

Hazel hadn't been up to lend a hand either and unless she had changed since her last visit I didn't expect she would help with anything involving syrup except the sampling of it. Hazel's idea of heavy lifting involves raising a full jug of syrup from the table to pour some onto a stack of pancakes someone else made.

By noon I felt I had earned my lunch and also a break. I was going to use it to track down Cliff Thompson and Karen Brewer like Lowell had suggested.

* * *

"Worst job I ever had," Cliff said when I asked him about being a library trustee. I had caught up with him at the fire station. The department, like so many others in New Hampshire, was staffed by volunteers. Cliff had served as chief for at least the last twenty years. Since his retirement he had taken to spending most of his waking hours in the station yakking with the other firefighters and playing solitaire on the computer. Which is handy since not only is he the chief, he is also the only full-time EMT in town.

"Because of the theft?" I asked.

"The theft made a tough situation even more complicated. The library was the real problem." I hadn't heard about this but that wasn't really a surprise. Gossip and troubles of all sorts flared up and died down all the time in Sugar Grove. Alliances got made, broken, and remade with every election cycle or new project that came into view. A thirty-year-old drama would have been pruned from the grapevine so many years ago most people wouldn't have remembered it had ever existed.

"What could have gone wrong at the library? It's a beautiful place."

"It ought to be with what it cost." Cliff's face took on a purplish hue and I wondered if he was going to need to practice some of his medical training on himself.

"I would have thought as a library trustee you would be proud of the place."

"That's just where you'd be wrong, missy. I became a trustee to help curb the outrageous spending in town. I was on the budget committee and when a vacancy came up on the library board partway through the term I got myself appointed."

"So what exactly happened?"

"Some folks in town got a bee in their bonnets about building a separate library building. They weren't satisfied with using a room in the town hall as a library and they wanted to put up a bond to build the one we have now."

"But you didn't want to?"

"Of course I didn't. The tax rates were already sky-high and that would only have made things worse. With a bit of renovation we could have continued to use that library indefinitely." New Hampshire has no broad-based tax and the property taxes are consequently a frequent point of contention.

"Did the other trustees want to build a new library?"

"Priscilla did. I didn't. Lisette Gifford was on the fence." Lisette is the pastor's wife. She tends to keep a lot of her opinions to herself, which seems to be a wise move considering her family's position in town. Being trapped between warring opinions from Priscilla and Cliff must have been rough for her to deal with.

"So how did you work it out?"

"I finally managed to convince Lisette that the families who were barely making ends meet needed to feed their kids more than they needed a new library. We approached the festival committee about donating the funds that year to the library renovation fund. They agreed and Priscilla got outvoted."

"Was Priscilla gracious about the defeat?"

"Nope. She's barely managed to look at me, let alone speak to me, ever since."

"Even though in the end the new library got built?"

"I don't think that helped any. There were some nasty words exchanged on both sides when the money went missing. It got so bad I prayed for a fire call before every trustees' meeting so I could avoid it."

"You didn't seek another term as a trustee?"

"It was too much aggravation. Before the end of the term I served I was popping antacids like peanuts. I'd still rather run into a burning building than tangle with Priscilla about anything again."

"Sounds like the money going missing really impacted your life."

"I didn't kill Spooner but I'd love to shake the hand of the guy who did." Cliff shook his head. "That man came into town all smiles and goodwill and ended up nothing but a thief and a womanizer."

"From what I've heard everyone liked Spooner."

"All the ladies liked Spooner. Even more than the men in town hated his guts." Cliff scowled at me.

"What do you mean?" Cliff was a devoted gossip who needed only the slightest encouragement to spill his secrets. The smallest push wrenched open the taps and all he knew gurgled out like water from the discharge end of a sump pump.

"Spooner roved his eyes over all the women in Sugar

Grove. He didn't even seem to have any preferences. From middle-aged married women to girls still in high school, he turned his charms on all of them." As aggravated as Cliff said he was, I heard a note of admiration in his voice. "If I had had a daughter instead of sons I would have locked her up until Spooner cleared out."

"That bad, was it?"

"Worse. That wretched man's disappearance was the best thing that could have happened to a whole lot of marriages in town."

"Anyone in particular's marriage?"

"Preston and Karen Brewer's, for one. Theresa and Gary Reynolds's, for another. Although, in the strictest sense they weren't married at the time, just engaged."

My heart sank. There was no way I wanted to poke my nose into the Reynoldses' private business. After all, I had finally managed to get their son, Mitch, to stop peppering me with citations. Maybe I could get all I needed to know from Cliff if I just kept asking the right questions.

"Was Theresa the high school kid you were talking about?"

"No, Pastor Gifford's daughter was the high schooler. Theresa had already graduated and was a contestant in the Miss Maple pageant."

"Spooner ran after the pastor's daughter?"

"I told you, he latched on to anything in a skirt. He sweet-talked Tansey into letting him live at her place, then was caught backstage at the opera house with his paws all over young Sarah Gifford on the Saturday of the festival."

"Did the pastor know?" I asked.

"Know about it? He gave the fieriest sermon I'd ever heard from the pulpit the next morning."

"He mentioned it publicly?"

"He certainly did. Service ran over by at least an hour by the time he'd gone into all the types of eternal damnation that awaited the men that betrayed trust and defiled innocents. Lust in the heart, that sort of thing. He was practically foaming at the mouth."

"Was Spooner there to hear the sermon?"

"No he was not. And a good thing, too. As worked up as he was just preaching to the choir, I hate to think how much worse things would have gotten if Spooner had been within the confines of the church."

"Did he manage to calm down at all?"

"If anything, venting his spleen seemed to make him more agitated. In fact, the deacon had to stand up and whisper something in his ear before he wrapped it up."

"Do you remember who was the deacon at the time?"

"Of course I do. It was your grandfather. Even he didn't manage to calm the pastor down. He just got him to finally sit so we could all get home to our Sunday dinners. I was grateful my wife had taken to using a slow cooker or else we would have had a cremated chicken that day." Cliff had given me a lot to think about. The pastor may have been a man of God but he was also a father. How far would he have gone to protect his little girl?

Eleven

Karen lived and worked out of a tiny lakefront cottage. Lots of cottages on the lake are year-round homes but many more are summer places only. Realtors like Jim Parnell call them three-season properties but most homeowners would confess they are lucky to get fourteen weeks a year use out of the places. Between mud in the spring and depressingly damp and frigid temperatures in the late fall it wasn't a place I'd want to be.

I chewed on a sandwich and an apple I'd packed while I bumped along the rutted track leading to Karen's. Most of the places looked devoid of life. Windows were boarded over on some houses to discourage partying kids or other sorts of critters while the owners were out of town. A lot of the summer people were from

Massachusetts or Connecticut and didn't come up to the lake outside of the summer season.

I passed only one house that looked occupied after I turned onto the private road that Karen lived on. It felt a little like one of those postapocalyptic movies where all the buildings are still standing but the people have vanished. I was glad to pull up and see Karen's car in the drive. I had called ahead to ask if we could meet but I was still happy that she hadn't been snatched away by some monstrous force.

"You're all by your lonesome out here at this time of year, aren't you?" I asked after she had taken my coat and offered me coffee.

"Yes I am, thank God. The racket all over the lake in the summer is enough to drive you nuts. Not that I mind the money, it's just the people I can't stand." Karen ran a property management business on the lake and disgruntled customers were part and parcel of things.

"I imagine some folks are hard to please."

"You wouldn't believe it. You know which ones are the worst? The people who feel guilty about owning a property they can't be bothered to use."

"I thought the lake was really popular in the summer." Lakes in New Hampshire tend to be full of people making merry on the water and along the shore when the weather was just right. If there was room to squeeze in a tent, or build even the tiniest structure someone would have done so.

"Oh, it is. But after a few years of ownership families

change. People divorce, kids get on with their own lives. It can be a real mess."

"That's too bad."

"Most folks aren't like your family with generations all wanting to keep the property in the family. The worst case is when old folks die and leave the property jointly to their heirs. Invariably a whole lot of ugly comes floating to the surface when some want to sell and some want to keep the place in the family. I can't tell you how much I hate my job."

Karen gulped a long swallow of coffee and thumped her cup on the Formica table. The whole place was decorated with a duck and boat theme. Everywhere my eye landed, crudely finished wooden signs said things like LIFE IS BETTER AT THE LAKE and FLOAT YOUR CARES AWAY. Karen didn't seem to be taking any of the sentiments to heart.

"Do you ever wish you were still the town clerk instead?"

"Every damned day." Karen leaned toward me, her eyes glowing like she had a fever. "That was the best job I ever had."

"You still miss it after all this time?" I had never considered how attached someone might be to a town clerk position but apparently I had been shortsighted.

"Health care, vacation days, clear and enforceable policies, an employee handbook. Of course I still miss it." Karen shook her head at me. "You know what I got now?"

"I almost hate to ask."

"Phone calls and angry people banging on my door at all hours. People who aren't happy with the size of their rental cottage. People who want to know why there isn't Internet access in the middle of the lake. People who want me to call an exterminator if a chipmunk crawls onto the porch."

"No wonder you miss the town hall."

"What I wouldn't have given to have kept that job. I hope you haven't bought yourself a property down here that you want me to manage. I only work for out-of-staters. I couldn't stand seeing a client at the Mountain View Food Mart in the middle of the winter."

"Nope. It's nothing like that. I actually wanted to ask you about your time as the town clerk."

"Why would you drive all the way out here to ask me about that?"

"Had you heard that Spooner Duffy's remains were found in the basement of the town hall?" I watched her face closely for twitching, lip biting, or other signs of discomfort. Karen just leaned in closer and let out a low whistle.

"I've been in bed for two days with a bout of stomach trouble and then I've been playing catch-up with returning phone calls and all that stuff that goes with running a business. I hadn't heard a thing."

"It looks like instead of running off with the money from the festival, Spooner never left Sugar Grove."

"Where'd they find him?" Karen asked. I told her about Russ and the coal pile and the spoons next to the skeleton. I didn't mention Tansey. "So what's any of this got to do with you?"

"My grandparents were distressed at how the renovations on the opera house have ground to a standstill because of Spooner's body. I thought if we could hurry up and get to the bottom of how he happened to be there we could get the job completed."

"Was the money with him?"

"Not as far as anyone can tell."

"Basements tend to be wet. I suppose the money could have rotted."

"I don't know about that. The opera house is set up rather high and everything seemed pretty dry. His clothes were in decent shape."

"But paper would probably take less time to decay than cloth."

"Maybe." It was a good point. I would be sure to ask Lowell if they had any way to analyze the body or the soil around it for decomposed currency. The paper for printing money was sure to be unique and it wouldn't surprise me if there were lab tests that could shed some light on Karen's question.

"Or, he could have taken the money and stashed it somewhere before he wound up dead. The guy had to be afraid for his life what with all his goings-on."

"What do you mean?" I pricked up my ears. Tansey, my family, and the doc had indicated Spooner was well liked. This didn't fit with what Cliff and Karen were saying about him.

"I mean he had an eye for the ladies. He didn't keep

his hands strictly on those spoons of his, if you know what I mean." Karen gazed off into space and crossed her arms over her chest.

"Doc MacIntyre did mention he was popular with the ladies."

"He was. But not so much with their husbands."

"Anyone in particular?"

"I guess you could start with my ex." Karen shrugged.

"I didn't know you were divorced."

"The marriage didn't last long. Being married to a policeman is never easy."

"Which policeman?"

"The old chief, Preston Byrnes."

"Sounds like a royal mess."

"Oh, it was. Jim Parnell came by the town office first thing to pick up the bank bag full of the festival earnings. The plan was for him to have left it locked in my office drawer the night before for safekeeping. He said that's what he did. When we got to my desk, it wasn't locked and the bag was gone."

"So who called the police?"

"I did. I rang up Preston at the station and Myra put me right through. Preston got to the town hall in under three minutes. My marriage was over almost that fast, too."

"Why's that?"

"Because as soon as Preston got there Jim said he knew it was Spooner who stole the money. When Preston asked him why, he said that I probably had mentioned to him that the cash was going to be in my drawer during some passionate pillow talk. Preston hit the roof and as far as I know never looked at another suspect."

"Wow. That must have been a bad day all around."

"It was. But you know what I never could understand? Why did Jim have to do that to me? He could have pointed the finger at Spooner without bringing me into it. After all, everyone knew Spooner had a key to the town hall."

"How did he even know about the affair to be able to tell your husband?"

"He saw us canoodling in the town hall when he came to pick up the key to my desk drawer. I guess I should have known better than to bring my private life into the office." That was probably what cost Karen the election. No one wants the town spaces being used for things that are best done at home. It probably put people off their suppers just imagining the goings-on.

"And you're sure the police never investigated anyone else for the theft?" Perhaps there was more hope for poor Spooner and for Tansey's image of him than I had thought at first.

"Preston and I didn't talk all that much about his work or anything else after that day so I can't swear to it. But, as far as I could tell, the entire investigation was focused on Spooner. Preston was obsessed."

"Did you two try to reconcile?"

"Preston wanted to after he had calmed down but I wasn't willing."

"Why not?"

"The way he acted when he found out about my affair really scared me. He got pretty violent."

"Did he hurt you?"

"No, but he did a number on the house. You know, throwing dishes, punching holes in the walls. I worried it wouldn't stop there so I left him."

"It sounds like you made the right decision," I said. As I drove away from Karen's place I had to ask myself if there was any way that the police had found Spooner all those years ago and if the chief had managed to make sure he wasn't ever found again. While it wasn't exactly what Lowell had authorized, I decided the next person I had to talk to was Preston Byrnes.

Twelve

Preston had been a fixture in Sugar Grove forever. Like my grandfather he had been born and raised here. When I was a kid I had found him intimidating and had been glad Lowell had replaced him as chief when I was still in elementary school.

Grampa always said Preston meant well but he came off as unnecessarily heavy-handed to most people. I had gotten the impression he enjoyed pointing out wrongdoing. Now I had to wonder if he was just an old grump because he was heartbroken over his marriage breaking up.

I was fairly certain I'd be able to locate Preston in his usual chair at the barbershop. He had far more freckles than hair on his head but he got Gus the barber to give him a trim every couple of days anyway. The days he wasn't getting a trim he sat reading the paper and looking out the plate glass window onto Main Street. I parked the minivan more carefully than I might have generally done since I could feel him eyeing me, measuring up the distance I'd left from the hydrant on the corner.

"Hope you're not here for a trim. Gus is off for the day," Preston said, laying his newspaper on the seat next to him.

"Why's the shop open if he won't be here?"

"Because I have a key and he likes me to sit in the front window scaring off the riffraff." Many years earlier some teenagers from out of town had tried to hold Gus up not realizing the old guy waiting for a trim was armed and always happy to be thought of as dangerous.

In short order three embarrassed kids were in the back of Lowell's cruiser and Preston and Gus were on the evening news. Gus has provided free trims to law enforcement officers ever since and Preston hangs out, keeping an eye on the place.

"I wasn't here for a haircut anyway. I dropped in to see you."

"What about?" Preston scowled at me. I sat two seats down from him and tried to look earnest and a little desperate.

"Hooliganism. I can't talk to Lowell about it because he's just too close to the family."

"Somebody in your family is kicking up a bunch of dust?" That got his attention. His ears started swiveling like an old-fashioned satellite dish. He snatched the paper off the chair beside him and patted it with a gnarled hand. I moved over and lowered my voice to barely above a whisper.

"Hazel's been out joyriding. She wrecked my car and did her best to corrupt a youth while she was at it."

"She's always been a rip, that woman. Was the kid underage?"

"Nope. That was the only saving grace to the entire incident. We're at our wits' end. I'm afraid she's incorrigible."

"Every year she manages to get up to some new sort of deviltry."

"Do you remember the year she led a naked toboggan team down the sled route?"

"Hard to forget a thing like that. The worst part was the way Hazel kept asking if I was gonna frisk her." Preston shook his head hard, like he was trying to rattle the image out of his eyeballs. "Something about the maple festival brings out the worst in that woman."

"That's just it. Hazel's shenanigans have got to be the worst thing to ever take place during the festival." I waited to see if he would take the bait. Preston wasn't a gossip like Myra but he was a born storyteller. Which is why he spent so much time at the barbershop. He had a built-in audience.

"You can take heart in the knowledge she hasn't caused the biggest stir," he said. I crossed my arms and tipped my head like I couldn't believe what I was hearing.

"I haven't heard of anything worse happening in my lifetime." And I hadn't either. Spooner was before my time so strictly speaking I was still telling the truth. I watched, pleased with my work, as Preston leaned back in his chair and laced his fingers together over his rounded gut. It looked like I might be here for a while.

"Maybe not during your lifetime but not long before you added your twig to the Greene family tree there was Spooner Duffy."

"The guy who just turned up dead in the town hall basement?"

"The very same. I knew he would come to a very bad end."

"What could he have done for you to expect him to show up under a pile of coal in the cellar of a public building?" Now I was even more concerned that Preston could have been involved from the way he was taking on a gleeful glow.

"He ran off with the earnings from the festival and left a string of broken hearts in his wake."

"Sounds like there should be a lot of suspects. Too bad he didn't turn up sooner."

"If we had known he was dead instead of gone I would have taken the investigation in a whole different direction."

"Was Spooner the only suspect in the robbery?"

"He was the only one missing. And he had a whole lot of reasons to hightail it out of town. Who better to suspect?"

"Lowell says the money wasn't with the body unless it disintegrated. And he sure didn't bury himself."

"Well, I couldn't have known that at the time."

"But now that you do know it, if you think back, was

there anyone else you would have questioned more closely?"

"Why all the questions about Spooner? I thought you wanted to pick my brain about your nutty aunt."

"You brought up Spooner, not me. And I hope everyone ends up being more interested in Spooner than in Hazel."

"I guess you have a point."

"So was there someone else you suspected?"

"I did wonder a bit about Jim and Tansey."

"What about them?"

"It occurred to me at the time that we only had their word for it that they ever actually put the money in Karen's desk drawer."

"No one else saw them go to the town hall?" That seemed hard to believe.

"Jim, Tansey, and a couple of other people were involved in the final tally of the take. Several people saw the money go into the bank bag but that's the end of it. I never managed to run down any witnesses that saw them going to the town hall or driving away from it either."

"Downtown Sugar Grove clears out pretty fast at the end of the festival. Everyone from out of town leaves altogether and residents are just happy to get home out of the cold. Just because you didn't find anyone who saw them doesn't mean they made off with the money."

"It didn't help put them in the clear, though, either. I'm not saying they did it but you did ask if I suspected anyone else at the time."

"What about Karen? She knew the money was going

to be in her desk and she probably had the opportunity to take it out before Jim got there. Did you ever suspect she could have had anything to do with what happened?" Karen seemed like a nice enough person but the last few months had taught me more than I ever wished to know about how people weren't always what they seemed.

"Karen said Jim was waiting for her on the town hall steps when she arrived at work that Monday morning."

"It would have been easy enough to come in earlier and then leave again. That way she could have pretended to discover the theft right along with Jim."

"Karen may have done some things I wished she hadn't and she may have even done some things she wished she hadn't but I can't see her taking the money. And I can't see her killing Spooner for it either. After all, she wrecked our marriage over the guy."

"You never married again?"

"Take some advice from an old geezer. When you find the right person, don't let him get away, because there may not be anyone who ever comes close to them again." Preston slumped a little in his chair. Without thinking about it I found myself reaching out and squeezing his hand.

"I'll remember," I said as I felt him squeeze mine back.

It was easy enough to approach Sarah Gifford Sparkes in a place where she had very little chance of escape. I am certain my grandmother was surprised when I volunteered to help out in the church nursery at Wednesday evening service. It was a task I had generally avoided ever since I was a teenager.

Grandma mentioned something about what people won't do to avoid their relatives. It was easier to let her think that I was going to the church to avoid Hazel and Jade. I certainly couldn't tell her about the favor I was doing for Tansey.

I knew talking to Sarah at the church was a great idea because she'd have a difficult time not answering my uncomfortable questions if she wanted to encourage me to volunteer again. On my way to the church, I turned over in my mind how to ask my questions. Despite the fact Tansey had called me a snoop, I really wasn't all that great at making people uncomfortable. I preferred to leave things like that to Myra or even Hazel.

By the time I arrived in the church basement Sarah already had her hands full with squawking children. A wailing baby perched on her hip and a toddler with a sippy cup clung to her leg. Three other preschool-aged children chased one another around the small room, leaving a trail of graham cracker crumbs and discarded blocks in their wake.

"Dani, your timing is perfect." Sarah thrust the crying baby into my arms. I jiggled it up and down and patted it experimentally on the back. It grabbed a fistful of my hair and began to tug. I can't say I enjoyed the pain but at least she had stopped crying.

"Does she always freak out like this?"

"She fusses nonstop every time her mother drops her

off. You can't turn someone away from attending church but I find myself hoping her family would move to another town." Sarah yawned extravagantly and collapsed into one of the two rockers at the far side of the nursery. "I really appreciate an extra set of hands."

"I was planning to drive Spring and Hunter in for their youth group anyway. I figured while I was here that you might like some help."

"I'm surprised you have the time, considering it is sugaring season and the festival preparations are in full swing."

"There is a bit of extra work to do for the festival now that Tansey is out of commission."

"I heard she took a tumble at the Stack. Is she still feeling poorly?"

"She isn't quite herself. You know she was friends with the guy whose body was found in the town hall?"

"That's hardly surprising. Spooner was really well-known around town."

"I never met him but what I keep hearing is that mostly he was friends with all the women. Even ones who were as young as you were at the time he was in town." I tried to keep my eyes on Sarah and her reaction to the conversation about Spooner but the baby kept moving her head into my line of vision. I couldn't feel irritated though. She really was awfully cute with her big dark eyes and cowlicked hair sticking up all over her head.

"I guess that's right. I know I was crazy about him but at least he was smart enough not to give any encouragement to the pastor's underage daughter. I was pretty heartbroken at the time but looking back, I'm grateful I didn't get myself into any trouble."

"Cliff Thompson said Spooner was spotted chasing you around backstage at the opera house at least once."

"Cliff does love a good story. Spooner was trying to get me to take a message to Theresa Reynolds. She was still Theresa Carter then, of course." Sarah shot out an arm and grabbed a little boy who held a wooden toy hammer poised above a small girl's head. "I told him I wouldn't and he kept following me around trying to convince me to do it. I ducked backstage to try to lose him but he followed me there, too. I expect that's what Cliff was talking about."

"What did he want you to tell Theresa?"

"He didn't want me to tell her anything. He asked me to give her a note." Sarah traded the boy a cracker for the hammer and sent him on his way.

"Did you finally agree to do it?"

"I did. I was so embarrassed by the scene he was causing that I took the note just to quiet him down. Spooner had a real thing for Theresa even though she made it clear she wasn't interested. He just wouldn't leave her alone."

"You didn't happen to read it, did you? If I had been asked to give another girl a note from a guy I had a crush on I wouldn't have been able to resist the temptation of reading it." I smiled at her, hoping enough time had gone by that Sarah wouldn't be reluctant to fess up.

"Of course I did. He wanted her to meet him at the

town hall the next night after the festival ended. He said he was doing some painting there after hours and that they'd have the place to themselves."

"Did you give her the note?"

"You know how when you are a teenager everything seems so important? Almost life or death?"

"I remember." Sarah was right. When I was a senior in high school, life felt so overwhelming and exciting all at the same time. Everything was suddenly too complicated and every choice felt like it had earth-shattering consequences.

"I did something I was ashamed of. I always looked up to Theresa. She was a couple years older than me, she was prettier than I was, and her family let her do things I never was allowed to do."

"I can understand that." Even though Piper had been my best friend since elementary school there were times when I had envied her. Especially in high school when she was so much more sophisticated at navigating the social scene than I had been.

"She had gotten engaged to Gary Reynolds only a few weeks earlier at Christmastime. Instead of giving the note to Theresa, I gave it to Gary and asked him to pass it along." Sarah squirmed in the rocker and I didn't think it was from the weight of the toddler in her lap. The memory still stung. "I guess I thought if Gary got mad enough he'd get Spooner off Theresa's back once and for all and maybe he'd turn his attention to someone else, like me."

"What did he do?"

"He asked who it was from and when I told him it was from Spooner he opened it right in front of me. I regretted giving it to him immediately."

"Did he cause a scene?"

"Totally the opposite. He got really quiet except from the noise of his jaw popping. The way he looked across the room at Theresa made me scared."

"Did he say anything else?"

"He thanked me for giving him the note and he said he would take care of it. He crossed the room and took Theresa by the arm and led her out the door."

"Do you think he hurt her?" I didn't know Mitch's parents well but with a town the size of Sugar Grove a lot of gossip made the rounds. I hadn't ever heard that there was anything but happiness between Theresa and Gary.

It was one of the selling points Celadon had pushed when she set me up with Mitch. Celadon seemed to think marital bliss was coded into DNA.

"No. I kept an eye out for bruises and that sort of thing for a few weeks but the two of them seemed perfectly fine. They married in August of that same year."

"I wonder if he ever gave her the note."

"I have no idea. But I can tell you I never saw Spooner again after Sunday night. I often wondered if Gary met him at the town office instead."

Thirteen

The next day had dawned cold and the forecast called for below-freezing temperatures. During my morning visit to the sugar bush there was very little sap flowing through the tubing and even less puddled up in the collection tanks.

Usually, once the sap started flowing I wouldn't have been happy for Mother Nature to put a halt on production. But with most of the day yesterday spent running around looking into the missing money I could use all the help I could get catching up at the sugarhouse.

Fortunately, not only had Loden been willing to fill in for me, the whole process of sugar making had become more streamlined with the modernizations I had convinced the family to install. For instance, just in time for the season we had added an automatic bottler and a filter press to the production process. Instead of hand-filling jugs with a well-balanced funnel or skimming impurities from the boiling sap with a mesh strainer we now had well-oiled machines to act as extra pairs of hands.

Even Grampa had admitted the changes were a good idea. Next year I hoped to add both a reverse osmosis machine and an automatic vacuum unit to our operations. As much as I had hoped to have added the vacuum unit to Greener Pastures already, now I was glad I hadn't gotten around to it. A vacuum unit helps to increase production even when the conditions are less than ideal.

The reverse osmosis machine would have been a help, though, no matter what. They remove seventy-five percent of water from sap before it even gets to the evaporator. Once we install one it will save countless hours of boiling time as well as the fuel that requires.

With the automation and the low volume of sap I decided that after putting in a couple of hours in the woods I could spare some time to pay a call to Theresa. I pulled up to the bank with a deposit bag and a box of maple-flavored saltwater taffy. It was still early, just past opening, but I knew Theresa wouldn't be able to resist my offering. She loves the stuff and who doesn't feel a bit of a craving for something sweet no matter what the hour?

As awkward as things should have been between Theresa and me, they weren't. Somehow, her son, Mitch, had managed to convince her that he was the one who decided we should break up. I guess Theresa thinks he broke my heart and she has been especially kind to me ever since. I headed straight for her teller window and slid the taffy across the counter.

"What a lovely surprise. You always were such a thoughtful girl."

"It's a bribe. I was hoping I could ask you a couple of questions and thought the taffy might make you say yes." Sometimes it is best to be subtle and sometimes it's best to cut straight to the point. I had too much to do with the sugaring to spend any more time than I absolutely had to on Tansey's mystery.

"Why not. You're the only customer. Come on into the break room. I'll have some of this while you ask your questions." Theresa grabbed the box and motioned for me to follow her through a side door into the back. Most banks wouldn't allow such a thing, I suppose, but since the bank manager had the good sense to realize the place would fall apart without Theresa he didn't even look up from his desk when she beckoned me through.

Settled at a table in the break room surrounded by the smell of burnt coffee Theresa unwrapped a piece of taffy and popped it into her mouth.

"I'm working on a commemorative booklet about the first fifty years of the maple festival and I wondered if you could help me out with some of the history of the pageant. I've gotten some good information from Jade but she said you were the person to talk to if I really wanted to know what the competition was all about."

"Jade said that? How sweet of her."

"Jade told me you were her idol when she started in

the pageant and that actually you were her inspiration for entering in the first place. She saw your picture in the family photo albums and hanging in the historical museum and she knew she wanted to wear that same maple leaf crown one day. To hear Jade rave about it I guess it must have been one of the best days of your life."

"It should have been but I always felt like the entire competition that year got overshadowed by all the chaos surrounding Spooner and the missing money. The speculation about that was all anyone could talk about for weeks. It was as if the rest of the festival hadn't even happened that year."

"Did you compete again the next year?"

"I couldn't. By then I was married and the competition is for Miss Maple, not Mrs. Maple. Although, Spooner almost messed that up, too."

"I heard about that from Sarah Gifford. She said Spooner was pursuing you despite your engagement to Gary." I hoped Sarah wouldn't feel like I was carrying tales but she hadn't asked me to keep what she told me a secret.

"He was relentless. You know, that guy wouldn't take no for an answer. I gave him no reason at all to think I was interested in him and he just wouldn't leave me alone. You know how it is with Knowlton making moon eyes at you every chance he gets? That's how it was with Spooner. I just couldn't shake him. It was kind of creepy." That explained a lot. It made it seem like

Knowlton's obsessive behavior in the face of rejection was genetic. I had more patience with him over the years than seemed logical. Now I felt like I had been right to do so. Maybe Knowlton couldn't help it any more than I can help being so short.

"So you must have been glad when he disappeared."

"I was. And in some ways I was even happier that he had run off with the money. If he had just disappeared I would have been worried that Gary had finally snapped and had done something to him."

"Because of the note asking you to meet him at the town hall?"

"Exactly. I thought Gary was going to throttle him. Gary is a great guy but he has always had a jealous streak. All those people giving me the eye during the competition didn't help matters. When Spooner started sending me flowers and notes I thought Gary was going to lose it. He actually went to the police to try to file some sort of restraining order."

"What happened?"

"Nothing happened. Preston told him not to bother the police department with something so petty."

"Did Preston ever question you or Gary when Spooner went missing?"

"He asked me a bunch of questions. As relieved as I was about Spooner being gone I was worried about the way Preston kept questioning me."

"You mean like you might have had something to do with it?" By all accounts, back then Spooner was Preston's only suspect. No one had mentioned the possibility of him having an accomplice. I should have thought to ask him that when I first questioned him about Spooner.

"That's exactly what I mean. First he asked me about the rendezvous I supposedly had with Spooner at the town hall. When I told him I never went he didn't seem like he believed me."

"Did he ask anything else?"

"He did. He had a bunch of questions about the bank deposit bags and who had access to what and when. He kept saying it was pretty convenient that I worked at the bank and that the guy who ran off with the money was crazy about me."

"But Spooner and the money were gone and you were still here. How did he explain that?"

"He said maybe Spooner had used me and that after he got the information he needed from me about the deposits he took off without me." Or maybe he was trying to divert suspicion from his own wife, Karen, by putting someone else in the hot seat.

"What did he think was the reason you would have been involved besides Spooner's interest in you?"

"He didn't really give me much of a reason. He didn't have to. I wasn't much more than a kid at the time and I was really intimidated about being questioned by the police. I was completely rattled by the whole thing and I think that just encouraged him to press me even more."

"Do you remember what he asked at all?"

"He wanted to know about the bank bags and who had them and if they locked and if I had a key. He had already questioned the other bank employees so I felt like he was just being kind of pedantic. Especially since I was still in training at the bank. I'd been there less than two weeks when it happened. That was until I caught on to the fact he was trying to get me to slip up about something."

"What did you tell him?" I asked.

"I told him the truth. I said I didn't know anything about the bank bag and that if he wanted to know about the festival and its banking he would be better off asking Frances. She had been on staff longer than anyone else including the bank manager. And she was on the festival committee."

"Who knew that the bag was going to be in Karen's desk drawer?"

"That would depend on whether or not the few people on the festival committee who knew about it told anyone. I just worked at the bank. I have no idea what committee members talked about." I had to bet that if anyone on the committee opened their mouth too wide they wouldn't have wanted to admit it to anyone.

"So what got Preston to stop bothering you about the theft?"

"I think it was when Lowell pointed out that I was out a whole lot of money myself since the check for the Miss Maple prize was being drawn on the funds that went missing along with Spooner."

"Did you ever get the prize money?"

"I did. About a week after the festival, when everyone had finally decided the money was not going to show up someplace Jim Parnell got to work and found an envelope full of cash shoved through the mail slot in his office door. It was marked 'Miss Maple Prize Money' on the front."

"Did you find out who donated it?"

"I never heard for sure but I always assumed it was your grandparents." That was the sort of thing Grampa and Grandma would have done, so her assumption made sense. I told myself to remember to ask once I went back to Greener Pastures.

Fourteen

I was eager to get back to work when I got home so I headed straight to the sugarhouse. When I entered the shop I noticed that thankfully, some-one had started a pot of coffee. I poured myself a cup and swirled a dollop of grade B maple syrup and a splash of cream into it. I wished I'd remembered to bring along some slices of Grandma's pumpkin bread to fill the empty bakery dome tucked next to the coffee station.

I blew on the coffee as I looked around. Despite the cold winds swirling around outside, the shop was cozy and warm. The woodstove in the corner was lit and the rocker in front of it beckoned but there was too much to do to sit myself down to work on the jigsaw puzzle we always left there.

Loden had been picking up a lot of slack for me and

it wasn't surprising to find him in the sugarhouse. What was surprising was finding him sitting at my desk in the office instead of standing over the evaporator. What was even more surprising was that the evaporator pan was completely empty. Not a drop of sap clung to its metal surface, not a whiff of sweet steam billowed from it.

"Not that I'm ungrateful for the way you've been pitching in all week but I was wondering why there's no sap boiling," I asked my brother. Loden tipped the chair back and looked up at me.

"Because there isn't any sap to boil down."

"What do you mean? It didn't go off, did it?" Sap needs to be kept cool or it will spoil. Spoilage of sap or evaporator pans boiling dry are two of the biggest concerns in the process of sugar making. Once the syrup is finished it will keep at room temperature almost indefinitely if a properly bottled container is kept sealed.

"Yes. Yesterday while you were off gallivanting." Loden looked surprised at my question. I couldn't believe it. All that work for nothing. Spoiling a batch was not going to win me any points with the grandparents and was sure to damage my chances of convincing them we should increase production. If I couldn't stay on top of the sap I was already harvesting there was no way I should invest good money in machinery that could help me waste more.

"How many gallons spoilt?" I hardly dared to ask.

"None. It went off with Knowlton when he came for it."

"Knowlton took our sap?" Tansey threatened not to

boil her own but I shouldn't have thought such a thing would have reduced Knowlton to thievery.

"Yes. He said Jade sent him for it with your approval."

"I never said Jade could help herself to a huge quantity of sap."

"Well, you hadn't told me she couldn't have it. And after all, she's a Greene, too."

"But how are we going to make any syrup without sap?" I couldn't believe it. Jade had always been high-handed but this was the absolute limit.

"The season's barely begun. There will be plenty more before it's over."

"Even if you're right, Jade should have talked to me before just sending Knowlton to take it."

"Right or not we don't need to keep an eye on the evaporator today. I'm going to the Stack. Do you want to join me for a late breakfast?" Even with my brain fogged over by irritation, it was clear why Loden wanted me to accompany him. My brother had been harboring a secret passion for Piper for years. He found it easier to talk to her when I was around to provide him with some conversational backup.

"No. I'm going back up to the house to try to catch Jade before she goes to work." I hurried out the sugarhouse door and into the shop where I almost bumped into Celadon's husband, Clarke.

He spends more time on the road than he does at home so finding Clarke at Greener Pastures always feels a bit startling. His back was to me and I was surprised to see a sprinkling of gray hair I hadn't noticed before. Clarke feels more comfortable in a boardroom than on the farm. Finding him in the shop had to mean something was up in the main house. Something unpleasant enough to make physical labor look like a good alternative.

"So what brings you out here?"

"I'm hiding." Clarke gave me one of the boyish smiles that had won Celadon's heart in the first place.

"From your wife?"

"Maybe a little. But mostly from Hazel. And from the conversations about Jade." I felt my stomach lurch.

"What kinds of conversations?"

"The ones that are cropping up all over. Celadon and your grandmother are upset by all the mess. Your mother keeps running around the house burning sage and mumbling under her breath. I finally came out here for some peace."

"Now you know why I like it here so much."

"If you're smart you'll have a pizza delivered right to the sugarhouse and just hunker down here until Hazel has blown off to wherever it is she gets to when she leaves."

"You know no one in Sugar Grove delivers pizza."

"Just one of the many reasons I love to travel. I could go pick one up if you want."

"No thanks. I'd better go to the house to see if Grandma needs me. Hazel's visits hit her really hard."

"I think I'll stay here and keep an eye on the shop

for you." Clarke winked at me then pulled out his cell phone and starting fiddling with it.

Clarke had been wise to hide. I found Grandma in the living room running a vacuum attachment over the drapes with enough vigor to bend the curtain rods. She had left three damaged ones in her wake. I thought about letting her know I was home but cleaning is the best tonic for her. She tends to think it is the best one for everyone else, too.

You know those mothers who feel cold so they tell their kids to go put on a sweater? Grandma was like that with cleaning. If it was making her feel better she was sure it would do everyone else a world of good. If you didn't keep out of her way when a fit like this came on you'd end up with blisters on your hands and calluses on your knees from all the scrubbing. I backed out of the room and right into my mother.

"Hold this," she said, thrusting a brass contraption spewing fragrant smoke into my hands. I stood trying not to sneeze while she pulled a bell from one of the many pockets in her long skirt. Mom began to spin in circles, ringing and jangling the bell. "Your aunt has picked up a psychic dark force."

"My aunt has always been a psychic dark force."

"She most certainly has not. Wave that incense burner over here." Mom gestured wildly into the corner with her bell.

"What makes you think she has picked something up other than a few new unsuspecting men?"

"Haven't you noticed how muddy her aura has gotten to be?"

"Sorry, Mom. I've been too busy with the sugaring and the festival to notice much of anything." Not to mention all the running around I had been doing for Tansey. But if my mother was as psychic as she thought she was she could figure all that out for herself.

"Your aura could use a bit of a buff-up, too, now that I am looking at you closely." Mom took a step toward me and rang her bell over the crown of my head with one hand and waved smoke from the burner into my face with the other.

"You're making me choke." My eyes started to stream and my nose stung. It was a wonder I hadn't developed asthma.

"That means it's working. I'd hate for you to end up with whatever is bothering Hazel clinging to you instead. Especially with all the things your father has been saying." Mom looked at a spot just beyond my left shoulder and winked.

"You've been talking to Dad again?"

"Of course I have. He talks to me. You wouldn't want me to just ignore him, would you?" Mom sent another puff of smoke straight at my face.

"I would never want you to be rude to anyone. Except maybe Jade."

"Your father was mentioning your cousin to me when

he dropped by. He was quite insistent about it. I think she's why he got in touch today."

"What did you see exactly?" Mom receives her messages in pictures and then interprets what they mean.

Unfortunately, her ability to communicate clearly with my father had not gotten any better after he died than while he was alive. My father was a taciturn man with a direct manner of speaking in the unusual event he had something to say. Mom was always trying to reach hidden depths and to add shades of meaning into whatever he said during their long marriage and she was still doing it.

From the messages he had sent through recently, I wasn't sure he had changed. Mom seemed to be doing just as bad a job of understanding what he meant now as she had in the past. I had more luck finding Dad's messages useful if I asked her straight out which images she had seen rather than accept her interpretation of them.

"You were standing here at Greener Pastures with a green heart-shaped stone pendant hanging from a leather cord around your neck. As you walked through the house the size of the pendant grew so large it pulled you off-balance and dragged you to the ground."

"That doesn't sound good."

"I wouldn't say that. Your father was smiling about the whole incident."

"What happened next?" I was sort of afraid to ask but I knew I wouldn't be able to get on with my day properly if I didn't. I didn't entirely believe in my mother's ability to communicate with my father but some advice he had supposedly sent over the last few months had proved insightful. At least after the fact.

Since I already felt Jade's presence like a millstone around my neck, I would like to have the opportunity for this to turn out better than the other warnings had. Or at least resolve itself earlier.

"You lay on your stomach and grabbed the stone with both hands. Then you pushed it out in front of you and scootched along behind it like an inchworm. You pushed and scootched to the doggy door in the kitchen."

"There is no doggy door in the kitchen or anywhere else in the house." Celadon had a dog allergy that made even the furless dogs an impossibility here at Greener Pastures. I'd lobbied hard for a hairless rat terrier once when I was about twelve. I saw one listed in the *Aunt Harriet's Swap and Sell* magazine at the general store. I pleaded, wheedled, and did extra chores for a week before I convinced my father to drive the family over to see if the dog just might not bother Celadon.

When we showed up it was the cutest thing I had ever seen. Without any fur it was easy to see large pinkish spots like polka dots covering its skin. Unfortunately, just being a few feet from the dog made my sister break out in some large pink spots of her own.

"This is why your father finds it so difficult to get in touch with you, sweetheart. The spirit world is not bound by the literal like you seem to be." Mom insisted my father regularly tried to get ahold of me but that I was simply not listening. I'd been trying but so far I hadn't seen or heard a thing.

"What happens with the nonexistent doggy door?"

"You wriggled on through and as you did, the pendant got caught on the edge and remained in the kitchen."

"And then what?"

"Then nothing. You wriggled through the doggy flap and the pendant just sat on the kitchen floor."

"Is Dad still here?"

"I'm afraid not. He said something about checking on the trees. You know how he loves to walk in the woods."

"So what do you think it means?"

"I think he is warning you about not buying oversize jewelry. It would overwhelm your tiny frame."

"What about the doggy door?"

"The complexities of your father's mind are sometimes too much even for me to explain. I have to confess to being completely baffled by that one myself." Mom plucked the incense burner from my hands and swished off down the hallway, leaving me with nothing more than a tickle in my throat from all the smoke and a nagging bit of worry tickling my mind. I followed Mom along the hallway and then headed up the stairs to my bedroom to look for Jade.

The door was shut, which was strange. As thrifty New Englanders the family didn't tend to turn up the heat. If I didn't want to freeze to death all winter long I left the door open in order to allow heat from the hall to drift in. I turned the knob and gave the door a shove. It took some doing but I managed to push it open.

Inside the room chaos reigned. I wasn't sure what had happened while I had been gone but I couldn't see the floor or even my own bed. The room looked like a large department store had exploded and my bedroom had been downwind from the fallout.

And it wasn't just clothing. Dirty plates and half-filled glasses, wads of makeup-smeared tissues, and even a clump of hair that looked like it had been yanked from a brush scattered across various surfaces. Over the pounding of blood in my ears I heard the floorboard in the hallway creak.

"If you think this is bad you should have seen the mess in the kitchen by midmorning. I wasn't sure I was going to survive the cleanup process." Celadon stood surveying the disaster. From the look of her hair, her halfway-untucked shirt, and the fact that she was wearing only one shoe, I was inclined to believe her.

I am not the world's pickiest housekeeper but I am particular about making my bed every morning and putting my clothes in the dresser drawers. I believe life is more enjoyable if living spaces don't smell like cups of soured milk and if every flat surface is not sticky with unidentifiable substances.

"If you're smart, you'll dig around until you find your pillow and a blanket and you'll move down onto the couch in the living room."

"Does it seem fair that I should have to move out of my own space because Jade is such a slob?"

"It may not be fair but it looks like the only safe thing to do. You're too short to be in there if the piles get any taller. I'd hate for you to smother in a sea of designer yoga pants."

"You don't suppose there's a dog under here some-where, too, do you?" I asked. Celadon's face flushed and she started breathing loudly.

"Why do you ask that?"

"Just something Mom said." I don't share Mom's visions with Celadon unless it is absolutely necessary. Celadon has had a psychiatrist on speed dial ever since she learned there was such a thing. When she describes our mother's mental health she uses words like *precari-ous*. I never like to make Celadon wonder if Mom is standing at the top of an icy cliff with a stiff wind at her back. I also don't really want her wondering if the same can be said about me.

I may not believe all of what Mom tells me but I am considerably more open-minded to the idea of life after corporeal death. I think Celadon never recovered from Mom telling her an elderly and recently deceased aunt had said hello to Celadon as she was having a bath as a small child. I'm not prepared to swear Celadon showers in a bathing suit. I will say her bikini is hanging in the bathroom to dry on a daily basis, winter and summer, and we don't have access to a pool.

"All we need is for Mom to start having one of her visions. You don't suppose she's going to try to rid Hazel of dark spirits again do you? The house smells like burn-ing grass for weeks every time she does that."

"I'm sure I couldn't say what her intentions are." Which strictly speaking was the truth. It was never a good idea to think you knew what Mom's intentions were. Besides, it had been a few minutes since I'd last seen her and they were likely to have changed since she relieved me of the incense burner.

"She had better not be out buying a dog."

"Why don't I go check?" I left Celadon standing in the doorway to my bedroom, peering suspiciously inside like something with a tail and a collection of fleas was about to wriggle out from under all the piles.

Grandma had moved on to vacuuming the couch when I slipped past the living room. From the way she was attacking it with the upholstery attachment I had no confidence there would be a sofa for me to bed down on even if I could have managed to locate my pillow and blanket. Maybe Clarke had been the one with the best idea when he suggested moving into the sugarhouse. I was thinking about check the attic for an old camping cot when my cell phone rang.

"Have you figured out who really took that money yet?" Tansey's voice was so loud I could hear it over Grandma's vacuuming. "Or are you on some sort of housecleaning bender?" I grabbed a jacket off a peg in the hall and headed out the door. The sun glinted off the snow and the smell of wood smoke drifted on the air. Out here, there was no sign of Hazel or Jade.

"You only just asked me to poke around."

"So?"

"So, the money's been missing for thirty years. It may take more than two days to get to the bottom of this."

"A smart girl like you ought to have no problems finding the truth about Spooner." I wasn't sure even if I did get to the bottom of the whole mess that Tansey was going to be happy with the results. I had no idea if she knew about Spooner's reputation with the ladies. She was a proud person and it might still sting after all these years. For now, I was going to choose my words carefully.

"I've been asking questions all over the place."

"Who've you been to see?"

"I talked to Doc MacIntyre, Lowell, Karen Brewer, and Preston. I've even spoken with Cliff Thompson and Sarah Gifford."

"And?"

"And, they all had things to contribute but nothing that could say for sure what really happened."

"That doesn't sound too promising. What do you have planned next?"

"I thought I'd talk to Jim Parnell since he was the one to put the bank bag in Karen's desk."

"Well, what are you waiting for? The festival is only a month away and if you don't want to be directing traffic, stapling signs to all the telephone poles, and ordering the extra Porta-Johns all by your lonesome you'd better get hopping."

"I have been hopping. You know I'm still boiling sap, too, don't you?"

"Get cracking, missy. Jim's bound to be around somewhere. Tell him you and Knowlton are thinking of buying a house together and that you want to see some listings. I

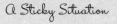

can have Knowlton meet you there to give the story some credence." The years it would take to convince Knowlton the house hunting story had all been an act did not bear considering. This needed to be shut down and shut down fast.

"If you want me to do this, I do it my way. I would rather work on my own. Besides, I thought you wanted Knowlton kept in the dark about the whole thing until we cleared Spooner's name."

"See, that's why I know you're the one for the job. Always thinking things through and putting the pieces together. With Knowlton's looks and your brains I am going to be a happy grandmother one day."

Fifteen

I drove all the way to the real estate office with the image of Tansey patting me on my bulging belly searing into my brain. I had to ask myself if it would be such a bad thing if Tansey sold up and headed out of town. After all, Knowlton was sure to follow her and my troubles, at least on that front, would be solved.

My uncomfortable chat with Tansey had given me a good idea of how to approach Jim though. I parked the minivan in Jim's carefully plowed parking lot and headed up the salted and sanded walkway. There was no doubt about it; Jim wanted potential buyers to feel at home.

The office was small and Jim had only one agent working for him. Sugar Grove wasn't big enough to support a large real estate market even with all the lakefront properties. He had a phone clamped to his ear when I walked in but he looked up and waved me into a seat across the desk from where he sat.

I plunked myself into the visitor chair and glanced around at the computer printouts of listings hung prominently on the walls. Big red banners proclaiming SOLD were outnumbered by listings stating EAGER SELLER or PRICE REDUCED. As idyllic as Sugar Grove felt to me, it shared the nation's real estate downturn. I hoped maybe that would make Jim all the more eager to talk about the old days.

He finished up his call and turned the full force of his salesman smile on me. "What a delightful surprise. Please make my day and tell me you've finally decided you need a place to call your own." He leaned across the desk, both hands planted flat on the gleaming wood surface. "I've got just the thing."

"I hate to disappoint you but I'm not looking to buy. I'm not even sure what it is that I'm looking for." I watched as his face stiffened into something I think he hoped looked neutral in the face of despair. "You do some business in rentals don't you?"

"I do when the opportunity arises. It's rare though. Are you looking for a house?"

"I was hoping there might be a small apartment somewhere in town. Right now I am sharing a room at Greener Pastures with my cousin Jade. The space is proving too small for the two of us." That perked him up a bit.

"Usually I wouldn't have any apartments in town but it just so happens Priscilla Martin's long-term tenant,

Frances Doucette, recently needed to move into Dappled Oaks assisted living facility."

"You mean the apartment above Stems and Hems?" Stems and Hems opened its doors before I was born and Priscilla has faithfully provided Sugar Grove with corsets and corsages year in and year out ever since. I couldn't remember a time when Frances had not lived in the apartment on the second floor of the shop.

I'd been in the apartment a few times as a child trick-or-treating and soliciting money for school fundraisers. I had loved the place so much Frances had a hard time getting rid of me whenever I showed up clutching a plastic pumpkin bucket or an order form. Unless something had changed drastically, it was exactly the sort of place I needed to convince myself to leave Greener Pastures and strike out on my own.

"That's the one. It isn't large but it's centrally located and it comes fully furnished." Jim tapped a few keys on his computer keyboard then spun the monitor to face me. "Here are some photos I was planning to use for the listing but if you think either you or Jade would like the apartment I can hold off posting it for a few hours."

"Could you show it to me right now?" I was looking for an apartment and I needed to stall for enough time to ask Jim the questions I came in for.

"Certainly. We could head over right now." He hopped to his feet and grabbed his winter jacket off the hook on the wall. "Just let me grab my car keys." I needed more time and I wasn't sure how much information he would be willing to share with Priscilla joining in the conversation.

"It's such a nice day. Why don't we walk?"

"Anything for a potential customer." He held the door for me and we were off.

"Were you the one to rent for Priscilla the last time it was empty?"

"As a matter of fact I was. I had just started out in the business. It had to have been more than thirty years ago now."

"Was the housing market good then?"

"You can always make a living if you are willing to hustle."

"Since you're still in business after all this time I guess that means you were willing to do just that."

"Boy was I ever. But you run a small business. You know what it's like."

"I do. My family has always helped with the maple festival but since I opened the sugaring business I've tried to use some of that volunteer time to get information about our products out there."

"I did the same thing. The festival is a great way to create visibility and to network. Why do you think after all these years I still do it?"

"Is it worth it? Some years everything just seems to go wrong," I said.

"You can say that again. When you are dealing with something so dependent on the weather sometimes there can be very little return on the investment of time."

"Like the year the blizzard blew in for the entire weekend and left thirty-six inches of snow in town."

"Or how about that time about ten years ago when

we had almost no snow to speak of and the temperatures that weekend reached into the upper sixties. We had to cancel about half the events because of a lack of snow."

"And now with Spooner Duffy's body showing up a lot of people are talking about how that was the very worst year of them all."

"Fifty years we've been holding this festival and that was the only time anything like that ever happened."

"Didn't anyone ever think it might be dangerous to leave all that cash in the town hall instead of dropping it at the bank? Lowell said it was twelve thousand dollars."

"It wasn't all cash. A goodly portion of what was raised was in the form of a check. We'd never had a theft like that before in Sugar Grove. I'm happy to say we've never had one since."

"That might also be because the festival committee probably never waited until the next day to get around to depositing the money again."

"Looking back, it does seem foolish. As soon as it happened I was pretty sure it was going to hurt my business when word got out about the theft."

"What did it have to do with you? Obviously, you haven't run off."

"No, but I was one of the few people who knew the money would be locked in the town clerk's desk drawer. I was worried no one would want to do business with the guy who was suspected of stealing from the library. Especially since it needed so much work."

"Cliff mentioned the library was supposed to receive the funds that year."

"That's right. The library was small and outdated. The town was divided just about in half over renovating the existing space or building something new."

"So feelings must have been running high."

"You should ask Priscilla about it. She was on the library board of trustees the year it all happened."

Sixteen

Priscilla looked up from the mannequin she was swaddling in enough tulle to hide a minivan. Priscilla's shop was filled to bursting with everything from galvanized floral pails to beaded evening bags to well-cared-for antiques. I couldn't help but run my hand over the dull sheen of the cast-iron antique sewing machine she'd displayed right in the center of the shop.

Priscilla had placed a basket filled with daisies and lilies on the treadle below the wooden cabinet. A length of pale pink silk draped under the needle as if the seamstress had been called away mid-project.

"Dani! Have you decided to come in for that dress fitting you've been promising me?" I had promised no such thing but Priscilla had been trying to get me to order a wedding gown from her for the past ten years. I was barely old enough to get married even with a parent's permission the first time she brought up my lack of a dress order. She hasn't failed to mention it every time she's seen me since.

"Actually, Priscilla, I brought Dani by about the apartment you have for rent," Jim said.

"I see." Priscilla paused. My guess was she was hoping I would fill in some details as to why I was interested in the apartment. Priscilla wasn't a gossip. I never heard her talking about anyone else but she certainly did listen and was always happy to tell you what she had heard about you. In my opinion it felt a bit like harassment and I wasn't sure I liked it any better than Myra's form of gossip.

"I told her it was still available." Jim seemed unsettled by Priscilla's lack of enthusiasm at my interest in the apartment.

"That would depend entirely on who was looking for an apartment. I don't rent to unmarried couples. In my business there is no profit in encouraging that sort of thing. No profit at all." Priscilla's face scrunched up as she gave her tongue a good clucking. Priscilla was all about the bottom line and I was betting that would get me the apartment, especially if I offered to pay a couple of extra months up front.

"Nothing like that. I'm actually looking because Jade has moved to town permanently. We are getting pretty cramped up now with the two of us sharing one small bedroom. Jim mentioned you had an apartment to rent so I wanted to come see it."

"Darling Jade. I heard she was in town. Do you think

she'll be in to choose some more dresses for your niece for the pageant this year?" My mind's eye flashed on the image of Celadon pounding on the bathroom door, promising Spring a pony if she would just come out. I doubted very much there would be a repeat performance of last year's shenanigans.

"I'm sure she'll be eager to chat with you about it just as soon as she gets her feet under her at the shop." In truth, it wouldn't matter what Jade talked with Priscilla about or even what she went ahead and bought. "Although I'm sure Celadon will want to take a look first and have the final say."

"I expect the Little Miss Maple pageant will have come and gone before Celadon deigns to visit the shop for a look." I heard Priscilla sniff. "Well, you aren't here to talk about your sister. Jim, you mind the store for me while I show Dani the space." If Jim was surprised by Priscilla ordering him around, he didn't let on. He simply nodded and took up a position behind the checkout counter.

I followed Priscilla to a warped wooden door in the back room of the shop. It was all she could do to tug it open even with the way heating systems tend to make doors fit more loosely in their casings in the winter.

Priscilla managed to heave the door open then motioned for me to follow her up a narrow stairway with a pitch that was more like a ladder than a stairwell. I had a hard time believing Frances had lasted as long as she had with such a climb ahead of her every time she arrived home.

"I'm not sure what you're looking for but it is furnished and heat is included. Speaking frankly, I'll be glad of the rent money. With the economic downturn people just aren't spending like they used to on flowers. Or on wedding dresses for that matter." Priscilla gave me a pointed look. "I've heard you've been spending a lot of time with that game warden from out of town lately. You aren't thinking of tying the knot soon, are you?"

"They're called conservation officers now and since he hasn't proposed I think it'll be a while before I need a wedding dress." Not that I'd be buying one anywhere. My mother was an enthusiastic and accomplished seamstress. She had made both of Celadon's wedding dresses and would be heartbroken if she didn't make one for me, too, if the time ever came.

"I suppose it's just as well. With your size we'd have to look for something from the flower girl collection anyway. Not nearly as profitable." I had to wonder if Priscilla ever listened to herself. The drop-off in her business might have had more to do with her propensity to offend customers than the state of the economy. "Well, here it is. Take a look for yourself." She pushed open another door at the top of the stairs.

I stepped into a living room and dining room combination. Set into a bay window sat a chintz-covered love seat. Built-in bookcases with glossy white paint lined one wall. Hobnail plant pots with ferns filled a white-painted whatnot shelf and a cheerful embroidered dresser scarf festooned a small end table.

"And through here is the bedroom." A white iron double bed covered in a seafoam green chenille bedspread and chintz throw pillows sat tucked under the eaves.

I was delighted by how cozy and pleasant she had made the space. Everything was built on a small scale. I felt completely at home. "And over here is the kitchenette and the bathroom." I followed her to the back of the apartment.

The kitchen was too small for both of us to fit in together so I entered alone in order to peek into the cupboards and the diminutive fridge. Vintage china and glassware filled the shelves. At the end of a short run of pink-tiled countertop sat the tiniest range oven I had ever seen.

Off the kitchen was a three-quarter bath with tile that matched the kitchen. Everything was tiny and cute as a button. I felt as though the apartment had been made just for me. As I stood in the living room once more I was seized by an overwhelming desire to rent the place.

"This space is truly charming." Priscilla's cheeks pinked and she smiled at me for the first time I could remember.

"That's sweet of you to say. Frances always said she thought of this as a life-size dollhouse."

"That's it exactly. I can see why she was here for so many years. I expect she misses it terribly."

"She does. But not as much as I miss her. I used to come up and have lunch with her almost every day after she retired from the bank. I checked on her most evenings, too, before I went home. I wasn't sure I had wanted to rent to anyone new but I don't think I'll be able to keep making the mortgage payments if I leave it empty. Besides, Jim convinced me it would be good to have someone else in the building again."

"I hadn't realized you and Frances were so close. She must have been good company."

"We were and she still is. I drive out to Dappled Oaks two or three times a week to take her books or some homemade treats." I was seeing a whole new side of Priscilla, one that was far nicer than the one I was used to seeing.

"That's really thoughtful of you."

"Dappled Oaks has a lot of amenities but a decent library isn't one of them."

"From what I've been hearing around town we're lucky to have a library that isn't worse than the one at Dappled Oaks. Jim mentioned on the way over here that you've been a library trustee almost ever since the year the fund-raiser money went missing along with Spooner Duffy." Priscilla pursed her lips and looked a lot more like the woman I was accustomed to encountering.

"That was not one of our finer moments as a community. But in the end it all turned out all right."

"Not for Spooner, it didn't," I said.

"Not for the library trustees either. To be honest, I thought before it was all over Cliff Thompson would have a stroke."

"He told me it was a difficult job."

"He thought it was. He didn't manage to last for

another term. All the fallout from the robbery was too much for him to take, I guess. Life can really be hard sometimes." She looked around the living room again, slowly shaking her head and straightening a throw tossed on the back of the love seat.

I could imagine myself sitting tucked up on the small sofa with Graham on the other end, a small, scruffy dog seated between us. In my imaginings we were carrying on a conversation with no one dropping in to see if he had popped the question. The vision I had created for myself was so appealing I heard myself speaking before I thought.

"Do you allow pets?"

"Frances had a dog for years. It wasn't any trouble, so I can't imagine why I'd object to you having one as long as it's small."

"You know, this is such a nice place I'd like to sign a six-month lease right now."

"Well, I suppose it would be all right. I'd much rather rent the place to someone I already know. I wouldn't want some stranger in here living above my store."

Jim called up from the bottom of the stairs to ask how I liked the apartment and if we'd made a deal. Priscilla jumped like she was a triple-bypass survivor caught with her mouth full and a half-eaten block of cheese in her hands.

"Are you all right?" I asked.

"I'm just very easily startled. I have been ever since I was a small girl. I get so focused on one thing that anything else coming into my attention takes me completely by surprise." Priscilla stood there immobilized, her trembling hand pressed at the base of her throat.

"Do you need some water?"

"I'll be fine in just a moment. No need to make a fuss." Priscilla held on to my arm as she led me out of the apartment and started down the stairs. "The more I think about it the happier I am that you'll be moving in here. In fact, the sooner, the better."

"What do you mean by soon?"

"Today, if it suits you. I'll just need first and last months' rent and a security deposit."

"That's exactly what I was hoping you'd say. I've got my checkbook right here." I dug into my purse and prepared to fill out a check for the first time in ages. Priscilla told me the expected total and then looked my check over carefully.

"I'll go get you the keys," she said. "And I'll make you out a receipt. You can never be too careful about the bookkeeping." Priscilla was meticulous about everything as far as I could tell. Her clothing had creases ironed into all the right places, her shoes could put your eyes out from the shine beaming off them, and her window displays were changed every Monday morning even if Monday happened to fall in the middle of a blizzard.

"Perfect." I stood there thinking about what I had just gotten myself into. On the one hand I was feeling that flutter of excitement that comes with a new venture. The world felt full of possibilities and opportunities.

On the other, I was not looking forward to telling the

family that I was moving out. They might be pleased for me and they might feel hurt. Probably, the reactions would be a mix of both. Priscilla returned, an old-fashioned two-part carbon copy receipt in one hand, a set of keys in the other.

"Here you go. It's all official and aboveboard just the way the taxman likes it. You can't be too careful, you know. If there's one thing a small business doesn't want to be ill-prepared for, it's an audit." Priscilla raised her hand to her throat again and looked around like she worried a government official might pop out from a corner.

"I know just what you mean. I'm very careful with all the paperwork at Greener Pastures. When I started the syrup business, that's one of the reasons I wanted to have an office in the sugarhouse instead of in the den at the farmhouse. The paperwork kept getting moved around and mixed up."

"Oh, you poor, poor thing. I had no idea." Priscilla placed a reassuring hand on my arm. "If you need to store some things here to keep them safe you are welcome to do so."

"I think I'll run the risk of leaving everything at the farm for now. There doesn't seem to be a lot of room in the apartment."

"Well, no, there isn't. But the apartment only takes up a small portion of the second floor. The rest is all storage. Frances used it and you're welcome to as well, but be careful. The floor's a bit rickety in spots. Now, if you'll excuse me I've got to get back to work."

Seventeen

 Even as aggravated as I was with Jade, upon closer inspec-tion the winery was still adorable. If I were being entirely honest I would have to admit I had harbored a hope that at a second glance Jade's execution of her idea would have been poorly managed. I wished that the good first impression it made had been purely based on novelty. That wasn't the case. If anything, the subtle details Jade had thought to include jumped out at me on this second visit.

I hadn't before noticed the way the bar rail and the upholstery tacks on the stools were a coordinating gleaming brass. Or the sparkling glassware on floor-to-ceiling shelves at the end of the tasting area. Jade had cards sitting on top of wooden wine barrels that suggested sap wine and cheese pairings as well as recipes calling for sap wine in the list of ingredients. I had no idea Jade knew anything about cooking. She had never lifted a finger to prepare a meal at Greener Pastures.

I wandered around looking at things all over the shop while Jade rang up a line three deep. Her chatty and friendly manner seemed to be a hit just as much as her products were and her sales reflected it, from what I was overhearing when she announced the total for each customer.

If I were being big about things I would have to admit I could learn a thing or two about retail from Jade. If I managed to swallow my pride long enough I might work up the nerve to ask her for some tips for the sugarhouse shop.

"It looks like business is brisk. Congratulations," I said.

"I haven't been in here alone even once all day. If this keeps up, the shop is going to turn a profit in the first year even if I take the renovation costs into account."

"That's wonderful." Only a couple of days in business was far too early to make that kind of prediction, if you asked me. But, if you asked me I would never have said a sap winery was an idea that made sense, so clearly I wasn't the expert. "You've been working some long hours."

"That's what it takes to succeed in business. But I don't have to tell you that," Jade said.

"It can be draining. You really have to do what you can to streamline the other parts of your life to make it all work."

"Absolutely. I've been cutting back on the amount of time I spend exercising and have gotten my morning routine down to under an hour." If Jade was spending less time on her appearance I couldn't tell. Every glossy hair was still hanging perfectly in place. The weak winter sunlight filtering through the windows bounced more radiantly off her face than it did off the stainless steel barrels holding sap wine. Even her eyelashes looked perky.

"It sounds like you are making a lot of sacrifices for your business."

"I am. But I'm sure in the end it will all be worth it. Especially with the low cost of the raw materials for my finished product."

"That's the reason I'm here." I took a deep breath and braced myself for impact. "I need to talk to you about the sap."

"What about it?" Jade crossed her arms across her chest and scowled.

"We need to reach some sort of understanding about how to make both our businesses work."

"Are you trying to cheat me out of the sap from the family trees?"

"I'm not trying to cheat you out of anything. I'm just saying you've decided to base your business on using a resource already set aside for another purpose without even letting anyone know you were interested in it."

"So what you're saying is that I should have asked your permission to start my own business?" Jade drummed her perfectly groomed nails on the gleaming butcher-block counter. I thought about how hard all the tapping and drilling and dragging of hoses and buckets were on my own nails. Not to mention all the cold weather chapping my hands. I felt myself beginning to lose my temper.

"I'm saying the sap doesn't up and decide to jump out of the trees and into some buckets for you to use. It takes a lot of effort to have any sap to use for any purpose. You deciding to help yourself to enough of it to run a second business without asking is simply not okay."

"The people collecting the sap are my family, too. There's no reason their effort should benefit your business more than mine."

"You're missing the main point."

"Which is?"

"I'm out there before anyone else drilling holes and tapping trees. I'm the one out on snowshoes at the crack of dawn checking miles of tubing for tangles and leaks. I'm the one making sure the sap remains at the right temperature to keep it from spoiling after it leaves the trees." With each angry word I felt more and more like the Little Red Hen. By the time I paused to catch my breath I half expected feathers to sprout up all over my body.

"You don't do that stuff alone," Jade said. If we were any younger I would have expected her to stick out her tongue at me.

"I may have the help of a lot of family members but

oddly enough, you're never one of them. If you want sap, go get your own."

"You can't be serious. You know I'm not the out-doorsy type."

"Then if you're not willing to pay for it you're not the sap-receiving type. And that's final."

"Final? You're joking. You know you'll never be able to stay mad about this. By the time we wake up tomorrow morning you'll be back to sneaking out quietly so you don't wake me up on your way out to check the trees."

"I won't be there in the morning. I've rented the apartment above Stems and Hems and I am moving in tonight." With that I hurried out the door before I calmed down and changed my mind.

"You want me to help you to move?" Graham's voice came through the phone loud and clear.

"I thought you might be happy to hear I'm getting my own place. After all, it means you can visit without running into Hazel."

"Well, that certainly has its advantages but I thought you loved living at home. Aren't you going to miss everyone?"

"I won't miss Jade or Hazel."

"What did your family say?"

"I haven't told them yet." I was still working up the nerve. I had phoned Graham from the car, sitting in a parking space in front of the winery. "I'll do it as soon as I get home."

"What time do you need me?"

"Does that mean you'll help me move?"

"Unless there is another exotic animal outbreak in Sugar Grove or the surrounding countryside, I can be there in a couple of hours." Graham rang off and I thought about how to break the news to the family. The only thing I could decide to do was to procrastinate so I headed to the police station to fill Lowell in on what I had learned.

Eighteen

Myra was in her customary place at her desk, yakking on the phone. From the sounds of things she was making a hair appointment with Shirley, the owner of the local salon, for a cut and color. She looked up from her desk where she was playing solitaire with actual cards instead of on the computer.

I tried to slip past her but she shook her head so hard her wagging jowls knocked the phone from its spot between her ear and her shoulder. She jabbed a pudgy, well-manicured finger at the visitor seat in front of her desk.

I looked at Lowell's closed office door and figured it was easier just to wait than to tangle with Myra. I sat and stared at the center of my palm, racking my brain for what my mother had once told me about the lines on my palm and my destiny. Nothing came to mind before

Myra finished her call and turned the full intensity of her interest on me.

"So, are you pregnant?" Myra leaned across the desk and scanned me up and down with her gaze like there was something in my face that would serve as a pregnancy test. As accustomed as I was to Myra's prying, I was still thrown off-balance by the question.

"Why would you ask me a thing like that?"

"Because you've rented Priscilla's apartment. I assumed your grandparents kicked you out for blighting the family name." Myra pushed a box of tissues across the desk at me like she was expecting me to break down any second.

"I am not pregnant and they did not kick me out. My grandparents don't even know I am moving out yet."

"Yes they do. Lowell's on the phone with your grandmother right now. You've made quite the stir."

"How did they hear?"

"I don't know that part. I just know your grandmother rang up asking to speak to Lowell. When I said he was busy on the Spooner Duffy case she said it was an emergency of the current sort and asked me to get him."

"And you asked what sort of emergency, I suppose?"

"Of course I did. She told me you were moving out to Priscilla's and I put her through to Lowell immediately."

"And your first thought was that I was pregnant?"

"Why else would you leave?" Before I could answer, Lowell's office door popped open and my godfather stood in the threshold. From the staccato motions he was making with his hand he didn't look happy to see me. I jumped up and hurried to his office. Even an aggravated Lowell was easier to handle than a curious Myra. He shoved the door firmly in place and sat behind his desk.

"What's this I hear from your grandmother about you running away from home?"

"How did you hear about it so fast?"

"Jade told Hazel and Hazel told your grandmother. Olive called here all dithered up. What do you have to say for yourself?" Lowell ran a broad hand through his thick gray hair.

"I wish I could have broken the news to them in my own time. But Jade always was a tattletale." I took a deep breath. "I don't like sharing a room with Jade because she's a slob. Now that she's started the winery it isn't like when we were kids and she was just here for a visit. But it's more than that. I've been thinking for quite a while about how it's time for me to strike out on my own."

"I see." Lowell drummed his fingers on the desk. "So you aren't moving out in a huff?"

"Is that what you heard?"

"Your mother says Jade told Hazel you were angry at everyone because you were forced to share your space with your cousin and had decided there wasn't room enough for the both of you at Greener Pastures."

"I know there is always room for me at Greener Pastures. But right now I don't think that's what is best for me. I'm ready to try something new. It's past time."

"Do you want me to call your grandmother and smooth things over a bit for you before you head home?"

"Thanks, but I think standing on my own two feet includes taking care of things like this, too."

"So asking for backup is not why you dropped in to see me?"

"Not at all. I will admit I was procrastinating delivering the news a bit but really, I wanted to fill you in on what I've been finding out about Spooner and the money."

"I hope it's more than I have." The deep lines between Lowell's eyebrows etched even deeper into his forehead. I wished my news were more illuminating.

"I'm not sure that you're going to want to hear what I found."

"Not liking to hear things is a policeman's lot. What have you got?" Lowell dragged a pad toward himself and grabbed a pencil.

"I'm sure it's not news that Spooner was a bit of a ladies' man." I paused while he nodded. "Did you know he was having an affair with Karen Brewer?"

"I knew the chief's marriage broke up fairly soon after the investigation into the missing money took place. I always thought it had more to do with Karen being offended at the questions Preston had to ask her about the theft."

"Jim Parnell spotted them locked together in a telling embrace at the town hall and when I talked to Karen myself she said the affair was what caused the divorce."

"And you think Preston might have been involved in what happened to Spooner?"

"I don't think anything about what happened to Spooner. I'm only interested in whether or not Spooner took the money, remember?"

"Good. Is there anyone else you aren't asking yourself about whether or not they were involved in Spooner's death?"

"I'm not asking myself if Mitch's father or mother could have done it." As much as I didn't want to I relayed what I had heard from Sarah in the church nursery about the note and Gary Reynolds's response to it. Lowell stopped writing and gave me his complete attention.

"This is really going to make Mitch uncomfortable."

"I know." Mitch and I had spent a lot of time making each other uncomfortable over the better part of a year. You know how teachers often live in towns outside of the school district where they teach? I think police officers should have a similar rule about dating. They ought not do it in the town where they are authorized to issue tickets and arrest citizens.

"You didn't bring this to me to get back at Mitch for all the citations, did you?"

"Of course not. Do you think I want to interact with Mitch any more than is unavoidable in a town this size?" Mitch and I had reached an uneasy truce and I hated to think about doing anything to reignite any bad feelings between us.

"I hope not. I hope part of your interest in getting an apartment is your relationship with Graham. If that's the case, keeping Mitch as far out of your life as possible would be wise."

"Are you going to repeat any of this conversation to my mother?"

"No, you have my word whatever you say will remain between us."

"Okay then. You yourself know what it's like trying to conduct a relationship with all the family watching. And now with Hazel doing her best to make Graham another notch in her cane it has become impossible." Lowell and my mother had been romantically involved for some time and it had not been easy for them, either, to carve out the privacy necessary for a relationship to flourish.

"If I didn't have a place of my own for your mother and me to go to for some alone time our relationship wouldn't stand a chance."

"Exactly. It's time to act like any other normal adult woman and be able to have guests and visits with those guests as I see fit without so much oversight."

"Enough said. Anyone else you think may be worth hearing about?"

"Karen Brewer had some worrisome things to say about her ex, Preston."

"She mentioned as much to me when I had some questions about Spooner's death."

"You talked to Karen, too?"

"Of course I did. I'm investigating a suspicious death. Letting you poke around about the missing money was not my way of shirking my duties." Lowell raised his voice a bit, which surprised me. We've always had a great relationship and I had to assume he was feeling stressed if he felt inclined to yell.

"I shouldn't have sounded surprised. And I shouldn't have made it sound like you weren't doing your job. I just got caught up in my own importance."

"It's okay. And I suppose speaking to Karen could have left you wondering about how much the Sugar Grove Police Department actually wanted this case solved."

"I did think Preston was less vigilant than he should have been but he couldn't have known that Spooner was dead, could he?" I kept my eyes fixed on Lowell's face. He took his time answering, which I understood to be a sign of inner turmoil.

"You stick to the money angle. If Preston had anything to do with Spooner's death I don't want you involved in the investigation in any way. It would possibly weaken any case I could build and it will probably put you in harm's way. So is that all of it?"

"Well, I was kind of wondering if Tansey reacted so badly to the news about Spooner's body being found because she was the one who hid it."

"I hate to say it but I thought of that, too. I can't think of a thing Tansey wouldn't do if she thought it was best for Knowlton and that would include murder."

Nineteen

My stop at the police station hadn't made me feel any less like dragging my feet about heading back to Greener Pastures. Now that I knew Grandma was upset I needed the sort of help only pie could provide. In my experience, pie cures just about everything. It fills up any wrinkles in the belly and fuels the brain.

It also makes sure you aren't talking since your mouth is full. Not talking can be a pretty good way to stay out of a lot of trouble. I wasn't fooling Piper though. She brought the slice of pie I had asked for on my way past the counter to my favorite booth at the back of the restaurant. She put the plate in front of me and held a can of whipped cream poised above the slice.

"Spill or there'll be no whipped cream for you." I made a grab for it but she was too quick.

"What makes you think there's something to share?" I asked, trying to keep my face cheery.

"You only order salted maple cream pie in the case of extreme emotional distress." That's the thing about lifelong friends, they know all your foibles. If they work in the restaurant business, that extends to your emotional connection to food.

"I've rented Frances Doucette's apartment and am moving out," I said, extending my plate toward the cream can. "Today."

"Not what I was expecting." Piper squirted down on the nozzle and unloaded so much whipped cream the pie looked like it had been in an encounter with the town plow. That's the upside to a lifelong friend in the food industry. They know when not to skimp on the good stuff. "Did Graham pressure you into getting your own place?"

"Nope. I did it to myself." I went on to explain how I had been thinking more and more often about getting my own place and the visit from Hazel and Jade had given me just the push I needed to take action. From the smile on her face I knew she was happy to hear that I was about to break my grandmother's heart.

"This is great news. There's no way you could invite Graham for a sleepover at Greener Pastures." She gave me one of her exaggerated winks that make men drive out of their way to stop for coffee at the Stack. It just made me squirm.

"I felt like I was having an out-of-body experience when

I told Priscilla I would take the apartment. I don't know what came over me. And right now is about the worst time of year to not be on the spot with the sugaring."

"The universe is kicking your butt. You've barely managed to get out of your own tracks since you moved back home after college. I think it's great."

"I hope it was the right decision because it's too late to change my mind now. You should have seen the way my hand shook when I handed Priscilla the check for the deposit." I took a bite of pie and savored the rich, sweet flavor and flaky crust as it shattered in my mouth.

"You've been home five years. You know I don't like to nag but it's time for a little acceleration in the growth department." Piper squirted a bit more whipped cream on my plate like she was trying to soften the blow of her words.

"I've been growing all over the place. Look at the sugaring business. Look at the maple cooperative."

"Those are all well and good but I'm talking about personal growth. Graham's a great guy and you could really use the opportunity to behave like a normal adult woman without worrying about the eyes of your grandparents landing on you like you were still fifteen years old."

"It isn't that bad."

"Of course it isn't bad but it is stagnant."

"So you really think this is a good thing?"

"I do. You just wait and see. You are going to absolutely love having your own place. Do you need any help moving, because I can have someone fill in for me?"

"Thanks but I already talked to Graham and he said he'd help me take over my clothes and personal items this evening."

"So you told Graham about the move before you told me?" Piper put her hand on her hip and faked a pout. "I'd say that tells you your relationship with him is becoming a really important part of your life. Yup, the universe is doing a bang-up job of getting you where you need to be whether you like it or not."

"You might be right."

"I'm always right. I'll come by later this week instead and you can give me the tour. I've always wondered what Priscilla had tucked away up there on the second floor."

"It's a date." I took another bite of pie as I watched Piper glide away to a table filled with men wearing power company uniforms.

Perhaps she was right. Maybe all of this was for the best and I would love living on my own. I just needed to work up the courage to tell the family. I thought about ordering another slice of pie to delay breaking the news but decided to show some personal growth and to head to Greener Pastures instead.

By the time I rolled into the driveway at Greener Pastures my nerves were raw. My emotions about having my own place swung wildly from exhilaration to sheer panic from moment to moment. Especially when I entered the kitchen and saw Grandma sitting in the old rocker with her eyes closed. For a second I thought the worst but her eyes fluttered open and she gave me an uncharacteristic scowl.

"It seems you've had quite the day, young lady."

"Are you angry at me?" I pulled up a chair from the table next to her and took her hand.

"Of course not. But I do wish you'd told us yourself that you'd been thinking of getting your own place. And for you to move out so suddenly feels even worse."

"It wasn't on purpose. I just fell in love with the apartment and after what happened with Hazel taking my car and Jade being here permanently I just heard myself offering to rent the place before I even thought it through. I didn't do it to hurt anyone. And I really think it is for the best. At least for now."

"What will we do without you?"

"I'll be here every day anyway. It's not like I'm moving out of state and I'm not going to start a sugarhouse at Stems and Hems."

"Hazel said you were moving in tonight. That doesn't even leave time for me to make a send-off dinner for you. Not that anyone else is home to eat it anyway."

"Where is everyone?"

"Your mother said something about spending the evening with Lowell. Celadon and her family went out to a movie. Your grandfather and Loden are at a poker game. Jade is planning to work late and Hazel left without a word after she dropped the bomb about your apartment."

"Graham's meeting me here to help me move. I'm sure he could be persuaded to put off the work until he's enjoyed one of your meals."

"That would be nice. But it won't be anything fancy." Grandma hopped up out of the rocker like she'd gotten her spirits back.

"Your 'not fancy' is my favorite kind of a meal." I gave her a smile. "And if no one else is here there's sure to be some leftovers. I wouldn't say no to a doggy bag as I head out the door." As soon as I said it I remembered what my mother said about me slipping out of the house through a doggy door and wondered if my leaving was what that image meant.

"Of course, my dear, I'll send you with a whole cooler full of leftovers. I expect there isn't any food in the fridge at the apartment and you know how worried I am about you starving to death."

"Are you sure this was everything?" Graham looked at the small stack of boxes and luggage on the floor of the apartment. "No more clothes or shoes or books or anything?"

"Clothes aren't really my thing." I had always hated shopping. At just barely four foot ten everything was always too long. Most of my clothing ended up coming from the children's department, which didn't really make for the best shopping experience. I stuck to the basics like jeans and plain T-shirts. With so few glamorous choices it was easier just to not bother with my personal style any more than I had to.

The entire contents of my wardrobe fit into two suitcases and that included my outdoor gear. I had an even worse relationship with shoes. When most of the dress shoes in my size were Mary Janes, shoe shopping was just depressing. I felt Graham staring at me and turned to face him. "What? What is it?"

"Are you saying no clothes is your thing?" I felt the hot rush of blood crawling up my throat and over my face.

"I'm saying I'm not a clothing enthusiast." That wasn't any better. Graham took a big step in my direction and pulled me toward him. "I mean, I don't like to shop."

"What do you like to do?" Graham bent low and whispered in my ear. It was late enough in the evening that his five o'clock shadow had grown in and scratched at my cheek.

"I'd like to give you the tour of the place." I pulled away from his embrace and took his hand. "Come, let me show it to you." I showed him the tiny kitchen and the even smaller bathroom.

"It suits you well. It's almost like it was built just for you." Graham took my hand and we headed back to the living room. "You look run off your feet. Shall we sit for a while?" I led him to the love seat and we sat, the quiet wrapping around us like an embrace.

"You know what's the only thing I can think of that would make this better?" Graham asked.

"No, what?" I braced myself for his response. We had all the privacy I could have wished for and I had even miraculously decided to shave my legs the night before.

"A scruffy little dog sitting here on the couch with us." I wasn't sure if I felt more relieved or disappointed.

But I was pleased to think Graham and I were on the same page about dogs. That's one of those issues that can be a deal breaker in a relationship.

"It's funny you should say that. I asked Priscilla about dogs before I took the apartment. She said it would be fine to have one. I've always wanted one but since Celadon is allergic to them we never had one growing up."

"How about once you get settled in a bit more we make a date to go to the local animal shelters and see if we can find a dog for you."

"That sounds like fun but are you sure you'll have time to go with me? You've been just as busy at work lately as I have."

"No matter how busy work gets I'll find the time. I have an ulterior motive." I felt my stomach flutter as Graham pulled me a little closer to him.

"Dare I ask what that is?"

"The way I see it, in order for me to reach my happily ever after you'll need to find a dog that likes us both." With that, he gave me the sort of kiss that makes your eyeballs go into a tilt, and then let himself out the door without another word. Living on my own clearly had its advantages.

Twenty

Grampa stood under the bird feeders filling a long tube-style one with thistle seed. Chickadees paid no attention to his presence as they landed on the mixed-seed feeder and filled their beaks. From their frenzied eating it looked like the weather report's prediction of a storm was liable to be accurate. The birds always knew when something was brewing and from the way the jays and other birds were hovering in the bushes waiting for us to leave I was pretty sure we were in for quite a blow.

"Need a hand, Grampa?" I asked. Grampa and I have filled feeders together in preparation for storms since I was big enough to pull on my own snow boots. I felt a lump in my throat as I thought about being in my apartment and not having any birds to look at as I sipped my morning coffee. Grampa must have been thinking the same thing.

"I've just finished. Besides, you're the one who needs the help, kiddo. Come into the barn and see what I picked up for you at the hardware store."

Grampa led the way along the path he had carved out with the snowblower between the house and the feeder and the feeder and the barn. He stopped to tuck the bag of thistle seed back in its bin and then made his way to a bench at the back of the barn.

"I thought you might need an apartment-warming present and I couldn't think of anything better than this." He handed me a paper bag full of something ridged and squared off. I stuck my hand in and pulled out a wooden and clear plastic contraption.

"Is this a feeder?"

"Yup. It attaches to a window and you can feed the birds from inside the house. I wanted to get something that you could see well up on the second floor. I thought without the birds you might be lonesome at your breakfast table."

"You always know just what to say." I put the feeder back on the bench and wrapped my arms around him. I felt tears filling my eyes and I was glad he couldn't see my face as he hugged me back. The advantage didn't last long. The more I tried to collect myself before he realized I was crying, the worse it got. Before long, sobs were shaking me hard enough to give me away.

"Do you remember that year when we were shopping

for plants for that flower bed your grandmother wanted us to put in for Mother's Day?" Grampa asked as he dug round in his back pocket and handed me a handkerchief. I nodded my head and scraped my face against the roughness of his coat. "I showed you that you should slide plants out of their pots in order to look at the roots before buying them. Do you remember why?"

I cleared my throat. "You said if the plant had been left in too small a pot for too long the roots would start to grow around in a circle because they didn't have anywhere else to go."

"And what was wrong with that?"

"You said that unless the gardener pried apart the roots and cut them a bit if necessary the plant would keep growing its roots in a circle even once planted in a hole in the ground. It wouldn't know any other way to be."

"Exactly. People are pretty much the same way. Your roots are important. They anchor you and support your growth but without a new pot every once in a while, you'll end up stunted."

"I'm already stunted." At least that's how it always felt when I tried to buy pants. Everything needed to be hemmed up by at least three inches or rolled so many times it looked like my ankles had spare tires.

"Not in ways that count, you aren't, but if you stay in this small pot for too much longer I'm worried you might be."

"So you think I was right to rent the apartment?" I pulled away and looked him in the eye.

"We all think it was the right thing to do even if it is a hard thing to get used to."

"Thanks, Grampa. I needed to hear that."

"Anything else I can do to set your mind at ease?" he asked. Grampa took the bird feeder from my hands and slid it back into the paper bag.

"Now that you mention it I did have something to ask you besides just whether or not you needed help with the bird feeders."

"I thought as much. So what was it?"

"I've promised Tansey I'd look into what happened to the money Spooner supposedly stole." I watched as Grampa grabbed hold of the end of his beard and started twisting it around the end of a gnarled finger the way he always does when he's agitated. "Don't worry, she told me all about her relationship with Spooner and what it has to do with Knowlton."

"Well, that's a relief. Some secrets feel like they're just itching to get out." Grampa dropped his beard before he managed to tie a knot in the end.

"And some don't. Like what really happened to Spooner and to the money. Which is what I wanted to ask you. Do you remember Pastor Gifford going over the deep end during his sermon the Sunday of the festival? Something to do with Spooner trying to get too friendly with his daughter Sarah?"

"I do remember that. The pastor was all het up and your grandmother was starting to make that leaky whistling sound. You know the one she makes when she's just about to boil over? I could hear her from my seat all the way up at the front of the church."

I did know the sound he meant. You know how the phone ringing at three in the morning or the sound of squealing brakes from the street turns a lot of people's blood to slush? For my family, Grandma's whistle noise strikes that kind of fear in our hearts.

I don't even think she's aware she's doing it. It starts out as a loudish sigh then morphs into hurricane-force winds pressed through a gap the size of a nostril. When you hear that sound, it is a sure sign Grandma is about to blow.

"I heard you were the only thing that saved the congregants' Sunday dinners from turning into burnt offerings."

"When your grandmother gets into one of those moods I'll do just about anything to turn her around and that includes cutting short a tirade I was sure didn't flow straight from God's lips to the pastor's ear. But what has that got to do with the money?"

"I was wondering if you thought the pastor was angry enough to have done something about Spooner himself."

"You're asking if I thought the pastor was angry enough to kill him and then hide the body?"

"Unfortunately, I am."

"He's far too sensible a man to lose his temper that way."

"Are you sure? What would you have done if you thought an older man was making advances to Celadon or to me when we were in high school?" I heard a gurgling sputtering noise get stuck halfway up Grampa's throat.

"Any man foolish enough to pull such a thing would have found himself running down the road with the seat of his britches full of rock salt."

"People in town think well of you, too, and wouldn't expect a man with your reputation to sink to violence. Why would the pastor be any different? He might have felt all the more responsible for ridding the community of someone he believed to be a moral blight."

"When you put it that way, I guess I can't say for sure whether or not he would have been tempted to violence. All I know is, speaking as a deacon who has worked closely with Pastor Gifford for years, I would be shocked if he was responsible for any of it."

"You were a deacon at the time, too, right?"

"That's how I happened to be near enough to him to step up and pry him off the pulpit. I was the deacon who led the opening part of the service that morning."

"Do you happen to remember any large amounts of money showing up in the church coffers at right about that same time?"

"You know, there were several large donations made to the church collection plate starting a week or so later. It was a lot of money and there was considerable debate about the use of it. Some of the deacons thought we should use the money for the roof repair fund and others felt it would be best used on missions projects. There was talk about dividing it up or lumping it together. By the time we'd worked it all out I almost wished no one had felt the urge to be so generous."

"How much money did it add up to?"

"It stretched over a couple of months but I think all told it added up to around six thousand dollars."

"Did you ever find out who donated it?"

"No one ever took credit for it and it was all in cash so there was no way to track it either."

"And no hints of any kind? Did you ever wonder if it could have come from the theft of the festival money?"

"It never occurred to me that the stolen money could be the source. Everyone, myself included, seemed to think Spooner had run off with that money. We wouldn't have kept looking for it in Sugar Grove."

"But thinking back now it seems like just about the right amount of money to account for what was stolen minus the checks they received."

"Do you think someone stole it and then felt guilty and changed their mind about spending it on themselves?"

"I think it could have happened that way."

"Do you suppose the robbery had nothing to do with Spooner after all?" Grampa asked.

"I have no idea, either about Spooner's death or about the missing money."

"What a sad thing to think a man has been lying dead all these years and no one ever cared about what happened to him." Grampa shook his head.

"At this point it seems like it doesn't matter all that much to anyone except Tansey. She took it really badly."

"As much as I hate to say it, it kind of makes you wonder if Tansey reacted so badly to the news about Spooner's body being found because she was the one who hid it," Grampa said.

"I've never thought of Tansey as the jealous type, but then, there haven't been any men in her life all these years besides Knowlton." I felt a knot tying itself up in my stomach as I thought about how Knowlton was likely to react if his mother went to prison. Tansey had spent half of Knowlton's first grade year sitting with her legs wedged under the desk next to his so he wouldn't sneak out of the building and run home every day. "Maybe she didn't want to risk losing her temper that badly ever again."

Twenty-one

 Dappled Oaks perched on a rise at the outskirts of Sugar Grove. There were indeed oaks all over the property but I was pleased to see a healthy sprinkling of maples as well. As I followed the winding private road into the senior living complex I was impressed by how well maintained the buildings were and how much care had been taken to create an attractive environment.

By the time I had parked the minivan in a designated visitor space I was no longer worried I would be depressed when I went inside. As I slid out of the driver's seat I thought about the fact that I still hadn't received news from Byron, my mechanic about the Midget. Sooner or later I was going to have to break down and call him whether I wanted to or not. But fortunately, I had more pressing responsibilities today. The view of the lake as I made my way to the front door was worth the visit all on its own.

The smiling woman at the front desk told me I'd find Frances in her apartment on the second floor. I was glad I had brought books from Priscilla as an icebreaker. I planned to use the fifty-year commemoration booklet for the maple festival as a cover story for my visit if I needed to. I raised my fist to knock on the door numbered 208 and steeled my nerves. Frances pulled open the door before I landed the first blow.

"Were you followed?"

"I don't think so," I said as she wrapped her small hand around my arm, looked up and down the corridor, and tugged me inside. I guessed her age to be around eighty and since I had last seen her she seemed to have shrunk a little in height and had lost quite a bit of weight, too. She pressed the door shut behind me and turned the lock.

"Good. You can never be too careful." Frances steered me to her kitchenette and waved me into a wooden chair. Priscilla hadn't mentioned dementia as the reason for Frances no longer living on her own but I had to wonder if she was entirely all right. Her eyes were slightly unfocused and she didn't seem to recognize me.

"I brought you these, from Priscilla," I said, handing her a shopping bag full of paperbacks in large print. "And this is from me." I presented a bouquet of delphiniums and hydrangeas I purchased from Priscilla before heading out. Priscilla mentioned those were Frances's favorites but I wasn't entirely certain the high cost of the flowers hadn't been the real reason for the suggestion.

"How thoughtful of you both. Let's have a cup of tea before you remind me why you're here. I don't know about you but I think best when well lubricated by Earl Grey." She put the kettle on and had even opened a package of store-bought cookies. But they were a fancy brand.

As much as I hated to admit it, even in the dark recesses of my own mind, store cookies were virtually unknown at Greener Pastures and as such were a luxury item. Grandma even baked her own version of fig bars. The only packaged cookies we ever had were animal crackers. And those were a rare treat for special occasions. I still love to eat them.

"Sounds delicious. I appreciate you making the time to see me."

"You look familiar. Shouldn't I know you?" Frances settled herself in the other chair and pushed the plate of lemon cookies toward me. I felt my spit spurt. The tea was good, too. Strong, hot, and in a china cup printed with little violets all along the rim.

But overriding the pleasure of the tea was worry about how far downhill Frances had been going. It had been only about six weeks since I had last seen her. Celadon and I had spotted her at meetings frequently over the years for things connected to the historical society. With the opera house renovation project under way we had seen her even more often.

"I'm Dani Greene. My sister and I have been to see you about the opera house restoration project."

"Oh yes, I remember now." Frances smiled at me but her voice sounded unsure. Her eyes didn't seem like she registered any recognition of me either. I wondered if the move to Dappled Oaks was the reason for her fuzzy-headedness, like the stress of the move had left her too overwhelmed to keep everything straight in her memory.

Even though I had come prepared with the booklet story now I felt crummy about telling her a fib. I decided one way to get information about the past might be to solicit advice on the present.

"I was hoping you could answer some questions about the maple festival and how the money should be handled. I am on the festival committee now and Tansey told me you were always so good at the bookkeeping details." Frances smiled at that and this time the warmth of it spread all the way to her faded gray eyes.

"The festival was always my favorite part of the year. So many happy memories."

"It is fun and I love it, too, but sometimes I'm worried about being in charge of so many details. Especially anything to do with the money. What if something were to go wrong and someone lost it or it was stolen before it got to the bank?"

"You are right to be worried. There are a lot of bad people around. Not everyone is exactly what they seem. The woman who runs bingo here used to work for the CIA, you know."

"I didn't know." I decided to stop in at the desk on

my way out to ask if there was someone checking on Frances regularly. Or if she was taking any medication that needed monitoring. "Did any bad people ever make trouble while you were on the festival committee?"

"Of course. There was the Realtor, Jim somebody, who really just wanted to use the festival as a way to market his new business. And there was Tansey Pringle, who was so bossy toward everyone else on the festival committee." Unfortunately, that still sounded like the Jim and Tansey of today. But why hadn't Frances mentioned Spooner? Surely he was the worst person to get involved with the festival over the years.

"Do you remember once, about thirty years ago, when the festival money was actually stolen?" Frances's eyes widened and then she nodded.

"I should have mentioned that straight off. Garland Duffy, but everyone called him Spooner, was thought to have made off with all the festival earnings because he disappeared the same night as the money. But I know he didn't leave town with the money." Frances hugged herself tightly and began rocking slowly back and forth in her seat.

"What makes you say that?"

"He was a good man and he loved this town and everyone in it far too much to do a thing like that."

"So I'm not crazy to be worried, am I? If the festival money went missing once it could happen again, couldn't it?"

"I would hope not but, I suppose it's possible."

"It's such a shame that people gave so much at the

festival and it didn't end up helping the way they wanted."

"The only saving grace was the number of checks people had written."

"I didn't realize the festival took checks. We don't take them now."

"People used to use checks for everything in those days. You know, when a purchase came to more than the amount of cash they had on hand or if they needed cash later for a place that wouldn't take a check."

"Were there a lot of them written?"

"For anything the festival committee handled or sold you could just make out a check to the Sugar Grove Maple Festival. Probably somewhere between a third and half the money was collected in checks."

"So, similar to how we take credit cards at the gate and for the raffles now?"

"I haven't been to the festival in a couple of years but I would guess so. That's not to say everyone took checks. The vendors up and down the street who sold food and souvenirs usually only took cash."

"How did the number of checks end up being a good thing?"

"Because when the money was discovered missing people rushed in to put a stop payment on their checks."

"But how did that help the festival fund-raising? Did the people who put the stop payments on the checks write out new ones to the festival?" I asked. After all, it was a matter of making an effort to do the right thing after the fact. And what about the out-of-towners that came? They would have had to have done a lot of digging to figure out where to send their donations.

"I was speaking more as a bank employee than as a festival committee member." Frances stared off into space like there was something she was trying to remember but couldn't quite manage. "I probably shouldn't mention this since it is bank business but since I was on the festival committee and worked at the bank I can tell you a lot more checks were stopped than reissued. And I could tell you who they were, too, if I weren't bound by my duty to the bank's patrons." Frances tipped her head to the back wall again and dropped her voice once more. "And because I don't want them to hunt me down for what I know."

I was definitely going to need to stop at the front desk on my way out. And I wanted to get to the end of the visit before she got even further out of touch with reality.

"Working in a bank must have burdened you with a lot of information about the folks in town."

"It certainly did. But that festival thing was very hard to keep quiet about. I had all I could do not to yell at some people when I stood behind them in line at the grocer or when I saw them at the gas station. As far as I was concerned what they did was no better than theft."

"I don't think I would have been able to keep such a secret as that. I would have been too angry."

"It was a question of trust and of loyalty. I'm sure you have secrets and burdens of your own that you carry, too," Frances said.

I thought about confidences shared and observations made, secrets ferreted out on purpose and by chance. I thought of my brother, Loden, and how I knew for certain he was desperately in love with Piper but was just not brave enough to show it. I kept his secret even though I was sure it was doing more harm than good, so I thought I might also have been able to keep the sort of secrets Frances held if the need arose.

"I always think of you as putting the good of your bank customers first. Which is why I'm wondering why didn't you take the money to the bank that night straightaway and put it in the night deposit?" That's what Tansey always did as soon as she could after the festival closed.

"Because we were too tired to count it all and make out the deposit slip. Besides, we'd never had anyone steal anything out of the town hall before and it didn't occur to us that there was any risk involved."

"It still seems strange now."

"Well, of course it does. Now we all know better because of the missing money all those years ago. But then we hadn't had that unfortunate experience. There was nothing wrong with what we did." Frances's eyes took on that faraway look once more and I sipped my tea in silence while I watched to see if she would continue. I was startled when she spoke again. "Do I know you?"

"My name is Dani Greene. I used to come into the bank and make deposits into my passbook savings account when you were a teller." Frances had been my favorite teller. She always made sure there were cream soda flavored lollipops in the dish at her window. Even if the other lines were shorter or even had no one on them I used to wait for Frances to be free.

"There were so many children over the years and so many Greenes, too. Were you the one who never did manage to reach the window by yourself?" Frances looked at my feet dangling several inches above the floor as I sat in a kitchen chair.

"Yes. I'm afraid it's still quite a challenge."

"Never mind, dear. I was always short myself. I always thought being tall was overrated. Although, I do wish this place was more like my apartment." Frances shook her head slightly as she turned her gaze about the small space. "It's tiny but tall, if you see what I mean." She pointed to the cupboards and the countertops.

"It isn't the same at all as the apartment above Stems and Hems, is it? Priscilla told me you always called that place your dollhouse when you lived there."

"I did, indeed. I loved that place with all its dainty furniture and cheery colors. I felt as if it had been constructed just for me. I hated to leave it but the stairs got to be too much for me."

"I'm sorry you miss it."

"The worst thing is thinking about it going empty and poor Priscilla being all alone there at the shop. She used to come up for a chat almost every night after the store closed. We used to have such fun playing cards and talking about funny things that had happened at work. Sometimes Doc MacIntyre would join us for a game of Yahtzee."

"That was one of the things I came by to mention to you. I hope you don't mind but I've moved into your apartment." A broad smile spread across Frances's face.

"How wonderful. Priscilla hadn't mentioned a thing. Perhaps she thought I'd feel replaced somehow." Or perhaps Priscilla had told her every last detail but Frances couldn't keep a hold on a short-term memory.

"I hope you don't. From what she's said, I know she misses you and feels you can't be replaced."

"I'm delighted someone will be there keeping an eye on her." Frances leaned in close to me and dropped her voice to barely a whisper. "And all the things I left stored when I moved here. There's almost no room in this place for anything. Except the listening devices." She motioned with her head toward the back of the room like she wanted to draw my attention to something hidden. I lowered my voice to match hers.

"There isn't anything stored in the apartment."

"Not in the apartment, in the storage area, which is also on the second floor. Priscilla was kind enough to suggest I leave all the things I couldn't bear to part with when I moved. Will you do me a favor and check that my photo albums are still there?"

"I certainly will if you want me to. Do you want me to bring any of them to you?"

"That would be very kind. I'd love it if you'd bring me the brown leather album with gold lettering. There's a scrapbook there, too."

"Where should I look for them?"

"In some cardboard boxes near the back, I think."

"I'll look for them later this week and bring them to you soon." Frances nodded then winked at me slowly like we had an understanding. She raised her voice back to a normal speaking level.

"How do you like the place?"

"I've loved it ever since the first time I saw it. Do you remember me dropping off amaryllis bulbs every year from the school fund-raiser?" Looking back, poor Frances must have spent all her pay during school fund-raiser months since every child in town was sure to have approached her and she never turned anyone away.

"There were so many children over the years. There was one little girl that insisted on coming into the apartment to make sure my order was exactly right. She never seemed to want to get on her way."

"That was me. Your apartment was so adorable and I felt so at home there I couldn't wait to go inside."

"I felt that way about it, too, the first time I saw it. That was my first place of my own, you know."

"I didn't know that." From my calculations that would have put Frances in her fifties around the time she got her first place. I felt my hands grow clammy.

"Yes it was. I lived with my parents until I was fifty-two years old. But despite a slow start I was determined to make up for lost time."

"What made you decide to leave home?"

"A man, of course. What else?" I suddenly felt like we had more in common than I really wanted to admit. At least I hadn't waited until I turned fifty-two to strike out on my own. Not that I wanted to share any of that with Frances. It was hard enough having the family tease me about it. "What's the name of your fella?" Frances reached over and placed another cookie on my plate.

"I made the decision to move out because it was time to try something new."

"Of course you did, dear. Just like you are here to drop off books from Priscilla. Who really sent you?" Her harsh tone startled me so much I gasped and a piece of lemon cookie lodged in my throat. For a moment I thought my life would flash before my eyes.

All I could think of as I tried to get the bite of soulless factory-produced cookie to move up or down was the shame it would bring to Grandma if I died while cheating on her baked goods. I grabbed at my tea and forced the cookie into submission with the power of Earl Grey.

"I can't believe they would stoop so low as to send you here to spy on me." Frances crossed her arms over her chest and started rocking slowly in her seat. It looked like the visit was going downhill faster than Hazel and her naked bobsled team. Time to change tactics.

"Don't you remember? I came to ask your advice about making sure money didn't get stolen from the maple festival."

"I don't remember anything about all that."

"Are you sure?" I leaned forward and tried to sound patient and encouraging.

"It's all very fuzzy. It must have been thirty years ago, at least." Frances stared blearily at a spot on the floor.

"There was a lot of trouble when someone disappeared from Sugar Grove without a trace."

"That sounds sort of familiar but I can't remember any details."

"I'm not surprised since there haven't been any details all this time. But something's finally turned up in the town hall basement. Under a pile of coal left over from the old heating system."

"And what was that?" Frances's eyes no longer looked unfocused. Rather, as she took a ladylike sip of her tea, her eyes looked like those of the mountain lion I had encountered a few months back. Large, curious, and vaguely like they would help with some pouncing.

"A body," I said.

"I hadn't heard a thing. What body?" Frances looked at me like she had just swallowed a fish bone.

"The one in the basement at the town hall. Russ Collins found it when he was working on the new furnace for the renovation." I was stunned that Priscilla hadn't told her all about it during one of her many visits.

"Do they know who the body belonged to?"

"People are saying it was Spooner Duffy." Frances's teacup slipped from her hands and crashed to the floor, splashing hot tea all over her lap.

"Get out. Get out of here this instant." She shoved her chair back with a screech so loud I thought the vinyl flooring was ripping.

"What did I say?"

"I never want to hear the name Spooner Duffy again as long as I live. And I don't care who hears me." Frances shouted at the far side of the room. I assumed she was making sure the listening devices could hear her.

"What's wrong?"

"You want to know what's wrong? Ask your damned Aunt Hazel, that shameless hussy." Frances grabbed me by the arm once more and pulled me from my seat. She yanked open the door and shoved me out into the hall. "Tell Priscilla I said thank you very much for the books." Then she slammed the door in my face so hard I thought my eardrums would pop.

It seemed no matter what I did it all came back to Hazel being a giant pain in my backside. I could feel Frances's eyes on me just peering through the peephole as I tried to walk with as much dignity as I could muster down the hall. I felt considerably less cheery as I retreated than I had when I entered earlier.

Twenty-two

Myra is easy to find and easier to get talking. Especially if you bring her a cinnamon roll with maple cream cheese frosting from the Stack. I handed her a take-out box still hot from the oven. Between bites, she was happy to tell me all about the feud between Frances and Hazel.

"Do you have any idea why Frances Doucette would call Hazel a shameless hussy when I mentioned Spooner Duffy?"

"Because he was carrying on with your aunt Hazel. Of course, she was already divorced when all the nonsense happened." From the malicious gleam in her eye I wasn't sure I wanted to hear anything else about Hazel but there was no stopping Myra once she got going. "I couldn't believe I'd see the day when there was a fistfight between two women over a man in the middle of Main

Street. Especially when both of them were over fifty at the time. Your aunt had a mean right hook, I can tell you."

"Dare I ask about the other woman involved?"

"Frances Doucette, of course."

"Hazel was duking it out with Frances in the center of town over Spooner?" I tried to imagine the look on my grandmother's face when she heard the news.

"By the time Preston rolled up in the cruiser, each woman was clutching a chunk of the other one's hair in her mitten. If it weren't for the bald patches I bet Preston would have arrested them both."

"Why didn't he arrest them?"

"He said he figured they'd both learned their lesson. It did them a sight more good to sit in a chair at the hairdresser than it would have to throw them in a cell. Excuse me for saying so, but I would have expected something like that from Hazel. But Frances, that came as a shock. Generally, she's such a proper lady. Almost too proper."

I had to agree. Frances might be a bit tart in her speech now but she never behaved in such a way as to call unnecessary attention to herself. She was the sort of woman in another era that would have been described as genteel.

"Did either of them say what they were fighting about?"

"Each one accused the other of stealing Spooner away from her."

"Were you the only witness to what happened?" With a town the size of Sugar Grove, I couldn't imagine no one pulled over to the side of the road to watch the action. After all, the most exciting thing to happen around here generally involved dramatic collisions between vehicles and moose out on the highway.

"Good Lord, no. Half the town turned out."

"Do you remember anyone specifically?"

"The Giffords were there and the pastor tried to break them apart, which is how I know about Hazel's right hook. Pastor couldn't see out of one eye for a week." That explained why my grandparents were so uptight about the way we all behaved in church. "Jim Parnell had a front-row seat and Tansey was so distressed by the carryings-on she sat right down on the curb and put her head between her knees like she felt faint and queasy." Or like she was pregnant with Knowlton and couldn't believe Spooner was seeing other women, too.

Once again I had to consider if Tansey's distress at seeing the spoons found in the basement had more to do with Spooner's body being discovered than it had at finding out he was dead. Was there any chance she had been the one to kill him? She certainly was strong enough and if she thought someone else might keep him from marrying her and helping to raise his son she might have been angry enough to do it.

I drove straight to Greener Pastures. Not only did I plan to ask Hazel about her involvement with Spooner but I needed to turn my attention to the sugaring operation. The weather had warmed up enough for the sap to begin flowing freely once more. More freely than information about the stolen money at any rate.

My first stop was the sugarhouse. The sugarhouse felt toasty warm with the evaporator chugging along turning sap into golden, thick syrup. When I was a child one of my first official jobs in the sugarhouse was as a taster. It's still my favorite part of the work. Dozens of squat jugs sat filled on the bench running along the long wall of the sugarhouse. The artwork on the labels brought a smile to my face like it always did. I loved the scene of the Greener Pastures sugar bush it portrayed. On the label there were bare sugar maples standing outside the sugarhouse, each with a galvanized metal sap bucket hanging on its side.

I opened the door of the firebox and checked to see if it needed more wood. I stuck in two more fat logs for good measure and then looked into the evaporating pan. After making so many batches over the years I could usually tell just by looking how close to finished the syrup was. Just to be on the safe side, though, I tested its doneness with a hydrometer. This batch still had a few hours to go.

I spent a little time in the office at the back of the sugarhouse shop checking e-mail and responding to queries. Bills needed paying, too, and then there was the business of checking the website for online orders. Creating an online store was one of the other ways we had increased our profits. It had been almost as tough to convince my grandparents a website was needed as it was to convert them to the idea of using tubing to collect sap. But in the end, even they agreed it had been a great idea.

After putting it off as long as I could, I decided there was nothing else to keep me from going to look for Hazel. I grabbed my jacket from its peg by the door and headed into the house. It was easy enough to find her. In fact, it would have been harder to miss her.

In spite of my grandparents' strict no-smoking policy I followed the smell of cigar smoke into the television room at the back of the first floor. Her cigar smoking was one of the many reasons she functioned as the family's patron saint of vices. When we were growing up, all any adult had to say to correct our behavior was that we were reminding him or her of Hazel.

"So here you are back again so soon after stealing off like a thief in the night." Hazel flicked ash into a candy dish perched on the arm of a threadbare chair.

"How could you possibly accuse me of sneaking off with the way you took it upon yourself to announce my business before I had the opportunity to do so?" I crossed the room and opened a window. If we could make it through the visit without Grandma having apoplexy over smoking in her home we'd all be happier for it.

"Don't tell me you were homesick after just one night away from home?" That was a cheap shot. It was no secret that several of the members of the Greene family suffered from severe homesickness, myself included. It had been so bad I thought I would have to leave college before the end of the first week.

"No, Hazel, I passed a very pleasant evening in my new place last night. Besides, you didn't think moving into an apartment meant I wouldn't be running my business, did you?"

"I suppose that wouldn't be your style."

"I've been at the sugarhouse working for the last couple of hours. When I finished up I thought I'd see if you were around."

"Looking for advice on how to handle that handsome devil of a game warden now that you've got your own place, are you?" Hazel leered at me and held out her cigar. "Want a puff? It'll do wonders for your bad-girl image."

"Actually, I'm here to ask you something but it's not about my love life."

"Well that's no fun." Hazel took another drag on the cigar herself and blew out a perfectly formed smoke ring.

"I was over visiting Frances Doucette this morning."

"Is she still convinced someone is bugging her house?"

"She mentioned there were some listening devices in her apartment."

"That Frances always has had the craziest things to say."

"Crazy is exactly how she sounded when I mentioned Spooner Duffy."

"She did, did she?"

"She tossed me out and told me if I wanted to talk about Spooner I should ask you. Now why would she say that?" I watched Hazel for any signs of discomfort. Not that I was sure what that would look like on her. I had never noticed her looking the least uncomfortable in any circumstance. She even managed to look triumphant laid out in the back of an ambulance when her attempt at being Sugar Grove's first human cannonball went horribly awry.

"Well, it might be on account of the dispute over Spooner we were involved in." Hazel shifted in her chair and I thought I detected a faint blush staining her cheeks.

"What kind of dispute?" After what I had heard from Myra I wasn't really in the dark but I wanted to hear Hazel's side of the story, too.

"It was of a private nature." Hazel slowly slid her hand up to her head and slipped her fingers under the brim of her fedora. She looked like she was checking something.

"Brawling on Main Street is hardly private." Hazel started moving her fingers like she was rubbing a worry stone.

"Frances didn't tell you that. Who's been filling your ears with tales?"

"I would have thought you'd have been crowing about it yourself. Especially since Spooner had to have been twenty years younger than either you or Frances."

"What can I say, those young fellers can't keep their hands off me. I bet your game warden didn't tell you everything that passed between us the other day at lunch." I was pretty sure she was right but I hoped anything Graham had held back was to keep me from mortification and embarrassment.

"Let's stick to Spooner. Are you saying you and Frances were both interested in him?"

"Frances was convinced he was in love with her." Hazel dropped her hand back into her lap. "Of course, he was actually completely taken with me. He never gave Frances a second look, as much as she wanted him to."

"Is that what led to you assaulting Frances on Main Street?"

"That's not how it went at all."

"Tell me how it did go, then." I sat on the ottoman opposite her and propped my chin on my hands like I had all the time in the world.

"I was minding my own business, just coming out of Bartleby's with a new sweater I planned to wear to the festival. Those alpine ski sweaters were very popular right about then and I treated myself to one." Hazel took a deep breath. "I had been feeling a bit low, if you must know, and thought a bit of shopping would cheer me up."

I had never even considered that Hazel could feel low. It was like hearing a glacier was spotted sliding across the Sahara. My shock must have registered on my face because she continued.

"The divorce had left me a bit off my game." Hazel's divorce had been big news in the family. Hers was the first anyone could remember. As much as Hazel had prided herself on doing just as she pleased for as long

Jessie Crockett

as I can remember, I'd heard she felt cruddy about the breakup of her marriage.

"I'm sure it was hard. From what I understand, divorce was a lot less popular than ski sweaters back then." Hazel looked at me and her face crumpled. For a moment I thought she would cry. Instead, she took another drag on her cigar.

"Everyone thought it was all my fault, of course. Because I was the one who did the leaving. It wasn't easy having everyone call you a hussy and worse. But it was the right thing to do. I couldn't have my daughters watching my marriage and thinking by my acceptance of the way I was treated that they ought to let themselves be treated that way, too." This time a trickle of a tear slipped out of one of her eyes and down the side of her long nose. She ignored it.

"It must have been pretty bad."

"Have you ever wondered why I'm the only one in the family who doesn't give you a hard time about not being married yet?"

I hadn't ever noticed but now that she mentioned it Hazel never did try to marry me off. Sure, she inquired after my love life but all she ever did was encourage me to have fun. I had always thought she was trying to inspire behavior that would worry my grandparents. Maybe she was really trying to keep me from the road she had traveled.

"Why didn't you ask the family for help?"

"I gladly moved all the way to California with that man just so my family couldn't see how he treated me.

I was too embarrassed. Being far away gave us an easy excuse to not be here for family dinners and holidays."

"It's hard to imagine you being embarrassed about anything." Which was true. Hazel was the most unabashedly brazen person I had ever met in my life.

"It was the incident with Frances and the sweater that turned me into the woman I am today." This, I had to hear. I watched as she snuck her hand up to her head again. "Like I said, I was coming out of Bartleby's feeling like I might be home to stay, even with all the whispers and rumors I had been trying not to notice. That's when Frances came up to me and started shoving me."

"How did that turn you into a devil-may-care rabble-rouser?"

"She said Spooner was going to marry her and I had better stop trying to wedge myself between them. She accused me of being used merchandise and said since I had already had one man I didn't see fit to keep ahold of, I should keep my hands off hers and any others that might be around."

"That doesn't sound like the Frances I knew when I was a child at all."

"I was surprised, too. It was like she was shouting to my face what everyone else had been saying behind my back. And then, she shoved me. I slipped on the ice and landed splat on my backside on the curb."

"How awful." I wouldn't have believed it if Frances hadn't given me the heave-ho out of her apartment.

"The worst thing was that my new wool sweater flew

out of the bag and into a slushy puddle full of salt and sand from the plowing. It was completely ruined. That's when I snapped."

I could see why. In the Greene family sweaters were prized. Many of the people in the family were accomplished knitters and everyone appreciated their handiwork. Sweaters, hats, and mittens were passed down from one generation to the next. That sort of treatment of a hand-knit sweater would have been too much to take sitting down.

"Did you retaliate?"

"I struggled to my feet and started shouting back. I said some things I am sure were not warranted and were certainly unkind. But I don't think they were bad enough for her to start in with the hair." Hazel looked like she was considering something carefully. Then she slowly removed her hat from her head. "Take a look at this." She pointed to a bald patch the size of a half-dollar.

"Did Frances do that to you?" Hearing Myra tell about it was nothing compared to seeing it for myself.

"She did. In a split second I went from scared to white-hot angry. Before I knew it we were both standing in the middle of the street holding clumps of each other's hair."

"The whole thing must have attracted a lot of attention."

"There was quite a crowd. I don't think I'll ever forget the look on Theresa Reynolds's face when she saw us. I think maybe that look is what made me come to my senses. It may have been for the best that things didn't work out for you with Mitch."

"Did you get arrested?"

"No. The police chief, Preston, was so busy sorting out the three car wrecks caused by the rubbernecking he just shook his head and sent us on our way."

"So what happened next?"

"Well, next I decided that if people were going to talk about me I was going to give them something worth talking about. And I wasn't going to be the sort of person who got pushed around anymore. Not by my ex-husband or anyone else."

"So that's when you started wearing fedoras and going on joyrides?" I asked.

"Absolutely. Hazel the Humble gave way to Hazel the Hellion. In some ways Frances did me an enormous favor." Hazel took another deep drag on her cigar then cackled wheezily. "I even ended up thanking her for it."

"When did you do that?"

"It took me a few days to work up the nerve. The new Hazel took some getting used to. I guess it must have been Monday before I approached her."

"How did she react to you?"

"She couldn't have been friendlier. She said she regretted what she said and that she hoped we could forget it had happened. She said there was nothing to keep fighting about anyway because she was never going to see Spooner again."

No one reported seeing Spooner after Sunday

evening. Was there a reason that on Monday Frances was so eager to bury the hatchet? Had she known for certain Spooner wouldn't be coming back? And even more important as far as honoring my promise to Tansey, how was she paying for her life at Dappled Oaks?

Twenty-three

It took some doing but I finally found Grandma in the basement dusting the shelves of canning jars full of her prizewinning pickles. Some of Grandma's best recipes are for things you put up in jars. I did a quick tally and noted with satisfaction that the shelf holding the maple pumpkin butter still held more than a dozen jars.

"How'd you find me?" Grandma asked. Taking a look at her, my heart gave a thud and landed in my fleece-lined boots. Grandma's cheeks were covered with dirty smudges.

"I looked everywhere else. When you weren't in the laundry room I figured this is the only other place you could be." I reached over and plucked a cobweb from the side of her head.

"Did anyone see you come down here?" Grandma

paused her flicking duster in midair. I was reminded uncomfortably of Frances and her paranoia. Maybe I shouldn't have moved out after all.

"No. I snuck down here as quickly and quietly as I could. Are you hiding from Hazel?" Grandma's shoulders stiffened and she started to shake her head then seemed to think better of it.

"I knew if I had to spend another minute with that woman Lowell was going to be visiting here on a professional call." I leaned in and gave her appearance a closer look. Her dress was spattered with something red, which I found myself hoping was not Hazel's blood. "Was there something you needed me for?"

"Well, there was but seeing you like this drove my question to the bottom of my to-do list."

"Don't worry yourself. As soon as Hazel gets herself gone I'll be right as rain. I just need to stay busy until she leaves. What did you need?" Grandma lowered the duster to her side and gave me her full attention.

"It's about an anonymous donation." Grandma is generally a truthful person but she doesn't feel necessarily required to share everything she knows just because someone asks. Even if that someone is one of her family members. Grandpa and Grandma are responsible for a lot of anonymous donations around town and throughout the state.

"Well, I'm not sure if I can help with something that's anonymous but I can try," Grandma said.

"I was talking to Theresa Reynolds about the money

going missing from the festival the year Spooner disappeared."

"What about it?"

"She said the prize money from winning the Miss Maple contest came from the festival proceeds and that with the theft there looked like there wouldn't be any prize money after all."

"I remember that. It was such a shame. But I thought it all came right in the end."

"It did. An anonymous donor left the money to make up the difference at Jim Parnell's real estate office."

"That's right. It's been so long I had forgotten but I remember now."

"She thought you and Grandpa were the secret donors."

"No, we weren't. We had decided that if it didn't all straighten out in a couple more days we would have done exactly that but someone else beat us to the punch."

"Any idea who it could have been instead?" I asked. Grandma never gossips but she does have a good read on the temperature of things in the town. It's a fine line but she managed to keep on the right side of it.

"If it was an individual, I can't imagine who it could have been except maybe Doc MacIntyre. He always had a soft spot for Theresa."

"I didn't know that."

"Theresa's mother was Doc's receptionist for years and Theresa's father wasn't usually in the picture. Doc filled in as a sort of big brother/young uncle for Theresa over the years. He wasn't really old enough to be a father figure then but he did what he could."

"Did you know that Spooner was chasing after Theresa even though he had a bunch of women already lined up?"

"Everybody knew about that. It was disgraceful. She was engaged to Gary at the time and they had such a bright future ahead of them."

"Do you think either Doc or Gary could have been angry enough to kill Spooner?"

"You know I hate to think ill of anyone but if push came to shove I think it's possible either one of them could have killed him. I remember your grandfather mentioning at the time that if Theresa were his daughter or fiancée he'd be tempted to hold Spooner's head down in the sap evaporator until he stopped breathing." Grandma gave me a meaningful look. "And you know how much it takes to rile your grandfather up about anything."

"Have you mentioned any of this to Lowell?"

"You know I don't like it when anyone carries tales, not even me." Grandma had a lot of patience for a lot of things but tattletaling was never one of them. But this was different from someone sneaking a cookie from the jar or putting toads in someone's clothes hamper.

"I think you'd better tell him. As much as I hate to think it, Spooner's killer may still be living in Sugar Grove and you wouldn't want that on your conscience."

"When you put it that way, I guess I'd best get in touch with him right away." Grandma gave a row of jars a final flick with her duster and headed for the stairs. "Even if I do run the risk of encountering Hazel."

Doc was at the Stack, looking over the menu just like he did every day. I figured it would be the perfect place to ask him about the anonymous money Theresa had received for winning the Miss Maple competition. I slid into the bench opposite him at his favorite booth near the front of the restaurant.

"How's the sugaring coming so far this season?" Doc asked as he stirred some calorie-free sweetener into his steaming cup of coffee. The Doc I knew didn't use fake sweeteners. I wondered if he had finally crossed the line into high-blood-sugar territory. No wonder he was curious about the sugaring this year.

"The sap is running pretty well. If this keeps up we might just have a decent year."

"Have you got enough help?"

"So far we're still managing with the family and a few seasonal employees but I think we're going to have to put a lot more trees into production to have sufficient sap to supply Jade's winery in addition to the sugaring business. That will probably mean hiring on some more people."

"It's always good to create jobs. There are a lot of folks in town who could use some extra money. You'd be doing the community a kindness if you grew Greener Pastures into a larger enterprise."

"Speaking of money and kindness I have a question for you."

"Sounds serious. Should I be worried?" Just then, Piper appeared at the side of the table and plunked a large plate of salad in front of Doc.

"There you go. One grilled chicken salad, fat-free vinaigrette on the side. Can I get you anything, Dani?"

"Anything but something as healthy as that." I pointed at the salad. I like to eat healthy foods. I happen to love vegetables in general and salads in particular but when I ate at the Stack I wasn't looking for healthy. I wanted crispy, gooey, or lofty and yeasted. The only way I wanted to eat vegetables at the Stack was if they were deep-fried and served with ketchup. Or if they came as a garnish or a pickle on the side of something meaty.

"I'll think of something and surprise you." Piper swished away, her vintage waitress uniform rustling as she walked. I thought about asking Doc about his salad but decided to hold my tongue. I didn't want to offend him before I even asked about the anonymous gift to Theresa.

"So what was it you wanted to ask me?"

"Did you give Theresa the prize money for the Miss Maple competition on the sly thirty years ago?"

"Why do you ask?"

"Because a whole lot of cash went missing and I am trying to figure out where any unusual amounts came from. Your name was mentioned as the possible donor of that money."

"Not by Theresa, I hope."

"No. It was someone else."

"Your grandmother?"

"Yes. She said you were protective of both Theresa and her mother."

"Your grandmother was right. It was me. I had low expenses and enough set aside for a rainy day that the prize money didn't make a dent in my finances. I hated to see that kid go without because of someone else's crime. Especially since she was planning on getting married. It takes a good bit of cash to set up house-keeping."

"But you didn't want her to know?"

"It wasn't so much her, as her mother and all the gossips in town. You know how people are."

"Why don't you tell me anyway?" I knew how I thought people were but Doc might have a completely different take on the local population.

"Theresa's mother was a proud woman with a strict sense of propriety. You know the kind of woman who would never let her daughter accept a gift of jewelry from a boy because she felt it implied a relationship beyond what was appropriate for a young girl?"

My grandmother had said some things like that when Celadon and I were teenagers. Celadon had a boyfriend who gave her a gold necklace with a heart on it for her birthday when they were in high school. Grandma told my parents they ought to make Celadon give it back because of the level of commitment it implied.

Mom just laughed and said not to worry. Dad took the boy to the den for a chat the next time he came calling. If I remember properly Celadon gave him back the necklace when they broke up a few weeks later.

"I know what you mean. What does that have to do with you?"

"I'm as close in age to Theresa as I am to her mother. Tongues wag too easily, especially if the family is the one to start in with the wagging."

"I see. You wanted Theresa to have the money because you felt concerned for her but you didn't want people thinking you had an ulterior motive."

"That's right. I especially didn't want to make things harder on Theresa than they already were. It was a crying shame the way her win at the pageant got entirely overshadowed by the fact that Spooner ran off and Preston kept grilling Theresa about possibly being an accomplice."

"She said she was pretty scared for a while. She mentioned Preston seemed to think she was the only suspect besides Spooner. I know if I were her I would have been worried." Just the amount of police scrutiny I'd experienced from Mitch and his campaign of harassment with parking tickets and moving violations had been intimidating enough.

"Preston did seem set on Spooner and Theresa being the main focus of his investigation."

"Theresa said Frances knew a lot more about the festival and the bank than she did. Why do you think he didn't grill her as much?"

"I don't really know. But if I had to guess I would

say it was a matter of pride. Preston never has been a man who was willing to be wrong or to offer an apology. Once he latched on to the idea Spooner and maybe Theresa were guilty he wasn't going to change course for anything less than rock-solid evidence that someone else was the culprit."

"Did you ever wonder if Preston didn't look too hard for Spooner because he already knew where he was?"

"Are you suggesting the chief of police had something to do with Spooner's death?" Doc dropped his fork back onto his plate with a clatter.

"I'm just asking. After all, from all accounts, Spooner had no compunction about laying his hands on every woman in sight. Preston told me his marriage broke up because of Spooner. He wouldn't be the first man to kill his wife's lover."

"Preston is not one of my favorite people. He's a blowhard and he wielded his power with more enthusiasm than I thought showed wisdom, especially in such a small town with so little dangerous crime."

"So you're saying you think he could have done it?"

"No. I'm saying the reason I didn't like him was he was too much of a stickler for the rules. I doubt very much he would have gone against them, even if by doing so he might have saved his marriage."

"I hate to say it but I've wondered if Gary could have been involved. After all, Spooner was overtly pursuing Theresa."

"He could have had something to do with it, I

suppose. He was a young hothead. And, he had recently been given access to the town hall."

"He did? Why?" That was news to me.

"He worked with the plumbing and heating company that converted the furnace in the town hall from coal to oil burning."

"Why would you know a thing like that?"

"Because Gary proposed to Theresa just after he got the job. He waited to ask her until he was sure he would be able to provide for a family. She was over the moon about the whole thing and it was all her mother talked about in the office for weeks."

"I don't want to think Theresa or Gary could be involved. They are both nice people. I really just wish there was some way Spooner could have accidentally buried himself under that pile of coal."

"And I wish you'd stop talking about unpleasant things while I'm trying to eat my salad." Piper appeared at the table once more and placed a plate in front of me. It was filled with something that looked like a cinnamon roll and smelled like a pasta dish.

"Chicken Alfredo pizza pinwheels and a side salad to keep Doc company," Piper said. "It's something new I'm trying, possibly as a take-out item. Tell me what you think." I thought about unrolling my napkin and pulling out the fork and knife but I wasn't sure how to attack Piper's latest creation.

"Is this a finger food or not?" I asked.

"I think that depends on your tolerance for mess. I'm hoping it will stay together fairly well, so why don't you try picking it up and biting it?" Piper pulled out her order pad and held her pen above it.

As relaxed as Piper is about most things, she's meticulous about recipe development and for her that means a lot of notes. If I had to guess, most of them are notes concerning my reaction to her recipes. Piper and I have been friends since before we finished losing our baby teeth. At least two of my loose teeth came out in some of her earliest creative efforts. I'm glad to say her candy making skills have improved over time.

I took a bite and was glad I'd left Piper to decide what to serve me. The bread was light and yeasty with flecks of basil and oregano. Swirled into the center of the roll was velvety Alfredo sauce, shredded chicken, chopped bits of spinach, and more cheese.

"I'll give it five smiley faces," I said. Piper nodded and scrawled a few notes on her pad. Ever since those first recipes we'd used smiling or frowning faces to evaluate recipes. Five was the highest praise available except for a smiley face with a halo. Which stood for a recipe so good you'd think you'd died and gone to heaven.

"Glad you like it. I've got some other flavors I'm trialing. I'll bring some by for you after work some evening when I come to see your new place."

"Perfect." I waved at her as she walked off to serve some customers I didn't recognize. I turned my attention back to Doc and the sad look on his face as he eyed my plate.

"So why are you eating that instead of something

like this?" I asked. Doc and I share a love of all things maple and also all things loaded with too much cholesterol. He prefers to eat the sorts of things a doctor who was interested in setting a good example would consume only in secrecy. Seeing him with a salad in front of him felt like I was sharing a table with a stranger.

"What's wrong with having a salad once in a while? It's exactly the sort of thing I recommend to my patients all the time."

"Are you feeling okay?"

"I've just been feeling my age lately and figured I ought to take some of my own advice."

"What brought this on?"

"If I had to guess I'd say it was the realization that Spooner Duffy went missing a full thirty years ago. Having his body turn up makes me feel my own mortality. After all, I've had at least thirty more years than Spooner did."

"And you think switching to salads might buy you another thirty?" I wasn't sure that was going to work out so well. If Doc's face was any indication of the stress he was putting himself under with every bite there was a good possibility he was drastically shortening his life.

"Only if they are a good thirty. Getting old is not for the fainthearted."

"So it would seem. Grampa and Grandma always seem so healthy and chipper. Even Hazel, as crazy as she seems, is in command of her faculties. But then there's someone like Frances, who can't remember from moment to moment if she's met you before."

"That's exactly what I'm talking about. You sound like you've seen Frances lately." Doc pushed his salad around with as much enthusiasm as a child who can't leave the table until he clears his plate.

"I saw her earlier today. She seems lucid one minute, remembering all the details of the festival and who did what and when. And the next minute she's completely forgotten who you are and why you're there visiting."

"I knew Frances's memory had gotten pretty bad but I didn't realize it was as far gone as that. They have doctors at Dappled Oaks and I'm not her primary physician anymore."

"Priscilla said the stairs were the reason Frances moved out of the apartment over Stems and Hems but by the time I had been visiting her for a few minutes it was pretty obvious something wasn't right with her mind."

"You mean besides the memory?" Doc stopped playing with his salad and gave me his undivided attention.

"She seems paranoid. She told me someone had installed listening devices in her room at Dappled Oaks and then she said the woman who runs bingo worked for the CIA. She asked me if I'd been followed and then later accused me of having been sent to spy on her. It was scary."

"Poor Frances. She was always a capable woman with a sharp mind. I never knew anyone who was such a stickler for details as she was except possibly Priscilla. Maybe that's why they got along so well for so many years. I'm certain it was one of the reasons she made such a good bank employee."

"I felt so bad when I left, I thought I would take her over some of the scrapbooks and photo albums she left at Priscilla's. Do you think seeing those might help her connect with reality a bit more?"

"It's impossible to say if they'll do any good and if they do, how long it will last but I don't expect it will do any harm. And another visit will probably be good for her even if she has no idea who you are. Laughter may be the best medicine but kindness goes a long way, too."

Twenty-four

 When I heard a knock on the apartment door my heart started thudding hard in my chest. I was still wearing the clothes I'd used at the sugarhouse. I hoped it was Graham paying me a visit and then I realized not only was my clothing filthy, the bed wasn't made and the dishes sat piled in the sink. I don't know if I was more disappointed or relieved when I opened the door to find Jade standing there with a tea towel–lined basket and a bottle of wine in her hands.

"I thought I'd stop by to check on you before I headed out of town. Something told me you might be up for some company." Jade flashed me one of her pageant-winning smiles and squeezed past me before I could make an excuse and close the door.

"What's in the basket?" I was still steamed at Jade over the sap disagreement. I wasn't above putting my stomach before my pride, however. As much as I wasn't thrilled at the prospect of spending any of my evening with Jade, my fridge was as empty as my sink was full. And even as delicious as the pinwheel roll at Piper's had been, it had worn off ages ago.

"Cheese and crackers, bacon maple chutney, and some chocolate bars." Jade plopped the basket onto the whitewashed trunk that served as a coffee table. Ever a slave to my taste buds I shut the door and fetched wine-glasses and a pair of plates.

"Letting you in here doesn't mean I'm not still angry about the sap," I said.

"I know. I've been thinking things over and realize I was being unreasonable," Jade said. Settling herself on the small sofa she peeled back the tea towel to reveal the treats inside. Jade expertly removed the beeswax seal from the bottle of wine and pulled the cork. "Let's drink a toast to fresh starts."

"Are you really prepared to make a fresh start? It feels like things are exactly the same as they were when we were kids. You show up here and expect to be treated just like the rest of us without having to pitch in with the work like everyone else."

"And you act like I'm an outsider that you're being forced to tolerate." For just a second I thought I spotted a crack in Jade's perfect veneer. I felt like I'd just keyed a brand-new luxury car. "And that you had to defend yourself against."

"When you put it that way I can see how I have been defensive," I said, feeling embarrassed at my lack of goodwill toward her. "But you always said things that made it sound like Sugar Grove and all of us weren't up to your standards. Like we weren't good enough for you."

"What did you expect me to do? You know the expression 'sour grapes.'" Jade let out a sigh and I thought she might cry. "Can you imagine how hard it is to see all of you getting to be Olive and Emerald's grandkids when I have to be Hazel's?" I hadn't ever given that any thought.

"From the way the two of you act I thought you felt she was the world's best grandmother," I said.

"Hazel and I are both outsiders. It seemed like a good idea to stick together."

"You know when I was little I just wanted my cool cousin from California to think I was interesting, too," I said. "But you never seemed to like me at all. I shouldn't have stopped looking to be friends with you."

"I think we really should try to start over," Jade said. "Especially since I'm here to stay."

"What did make you decide to open the winery? I thought your heart belonged to the pageant business." By all accounts Jade was one of the leading pageant coaches in the country. Why she would have abandoned a thriving business in a field she loved was as baffling as what had happened to the missing festival money.

I spread some of the chutney onto a cracker and popped it into my mouth. The combination was sweet and salty with a hint of apple and onion. I reached for another and then some cheese before I noticed Jade wasn't tucking in along with me.

"Would you believe me if I said I needed a change of pace?" Jade asked.

"Not at all. You were always so passionate about competition and sharing what you knew about winning with younger people. Look how involved you got last year trying to turn Spring into a Little Miss Maple champion," I said. "I think you wanted her to win far more than she wanted it herself."

"That's the problem. Sometimes I go a bit overboard," Jade said.

"But I thought you once said the key to winning was remembering that too much was never enough."

"Turns out I was wrong about that." Jade pulled the throw off the back of the sofa and wrapped it around herself like she was trying to hide from something. "My coaching business went kaput."

"What happened?" I asked.

"There was an incident." Jade slouched deeper into the sofa and for once she didn't look like she had all the answers. As much as I would have expected to be happy to hear she wasn't perfect I couldn't help but feel sorry for her.

"That doesn't sound good." I reached into the basket, pulled out a chocolate bar, and handed her a piece.

"Let's just say by the end of it there was no question that I had descended from Hazel's branch of the family instead of your grandmother's."

"Did you get arrested?" In my mind Hazel incidents and arrests were something that went together like waffles and syrup.

"No, but I was run out of the business by a judge," Jade said.

"I don't think Hazel has ever gone that far. How did you manage that?"

"I overreached. I pushed too hard. I thought I had finally found a competitor who could end up being Miss America one day."

"That doesn't sound like something that should involve the legal profession."

"Not that kind of judge. A pageant judge. She got it into her head to give low marks to every one of my clients."

"Why would she do a thing like that?" It didn't make sense. People inexplicably liked Jade the way they liked fad purchases like pet rocks and beanbag stuffed toys. No one except Celadon and I ever seemed to dislike her.

"I choreographed a routine involving flaming batons for my very talented young competitor. Unfortunately, I didn't take into account the fact she suffered from severe allergies."

"Not following you."

"Congestion in her head threw off her balance. I thought she was ready for four-inch heels but looking back on it I guess her mother was right when she said the child was too young for them."

"How old was she?"

"Six. But in my defense she looked twelve. Especially in the heels."

"Did the judge not approve of the heels either?" I thought it best not to weigh in on the subject of heels and age appropriateness if we were trying to make up. Even with my burning desire to be taller than four foot ten I couldn't attempt such high heels. And I was twenty-seven.

"It wasn't the heels so much as the tripping and the flaming batons. What I don't understand is why she had to be so spiteful about it. After the judge's surgery you could barely notice the scarring at all." Jade shook her head and sighed deeply. "She gave such low marks to each one of my clients once she was back on the judging circuit that having me as a coach became a total liability. Before a year was out my business had gone completely under."

"So naturally, you decided to open a winery?" I asked.

"Why not? I'm just following in my parents' footsteps."

"But why would you come to Sugar Grove if you wanted to follow your parents into the wine business? Wouldn't it have been far better to stay in California and to stick to wines made from grapes?" Not that I would ever have anything bad to say about what might be made from sap but it was an obvious question.

"Because I was inspired by you. You're making a success of your business and you've made working in Sugar Grove seem like such fun I thought I would give it a go myself. Besides, sap wine is not exactly a household name and I decided I would enjoy the challenge of trying to make it one."

"I won't argue with you about the merits of all things maple." I bit into a piece of maple bacon cheddar.

"But you will argue with me about the sap. I know I shouldn't have sent Knowlton over to get it without talking to you about it first but I didn't do it for the reasons you think." Jade took a long sip of her wine and then sagged back against the sofa.

"You didn't hijack my sap in order to produce wine for your own business? What other reason could you possibly have had?"

"I had to get rid of Knowlton." That explained it. Knowlton's passion for any of the Greene girls was like a chronic illness.

The only real relief we seemed to get from his fervent pursuit was when Jade came to town. It was the one thing I had always enjoyed about her visits. Now with her moving to Sugar Grove full-time surely his attention to me would be lessened.

"He can be hard to take."

"'Hard to take' doesn't begin to describe it. Do you know he's started waiting for me on the front steps of the winery every morning when I arrive?" That explained why he wasn't skulking around the sugar bush waiting to pounce on me each morning as I checked how the sap was flowing.

"It's nice to see a friendly face."

"He stays all day. I can't seem to get rid of him. He

parks himself at the tasting counter and yaks my ear off all day long about taxidermy." Jade plucked an apricot from the basket and bit down on it with enough force to snap a perfectly whitened tooth.

"So you decided if you couldn't get rid of him you could put him to work? There must be something else you could have had him do to be helpful. Running errands, that sort of thing."

"I tried but he wasn't taking the hint, wouldn't consider budging until I mentioned visiting Greener Pastures." Jade threw off the blanket she'd cocooned herself in and stood.

"So you sent him to me?" I paused, a bit of chocolate halfway to my lips. "That wasn't a great way to get on my good side."

"I was desperate. Yesterday morning he told me how he would pose me if I were stuffed."

"I'm sure he meant it as a compliment," I said.

"I don't see how."

"I expect he wanted to preserve your lifelike beauty."

I had to agree with her about the creepiness. I had often suspected some of Knowlton's daydreams involved posing Celadon and me in cheerful domestic scenes neither of us would have participated in while alive. I wondered if he was just so enraptured with Jade that he completely forgot himself or if the situation with Tansey had sent him over the edge.

"He's driving me batty. It's almost enough to make me regret opening the winery." Jade poured herself another glass of wine and looked like she was prepared to drown her sorrows.

"So you hadn't factored him into your business plan?"

"No. He was not any part of any of my plans. With the way he has been talking taxidermy at the winery I'm afraid he is going to drive off business. Roadkill is hardly the sort of pairing I had in mind for my wines."

"So what you really want is to be able to send Knowlton on a sap-collecting run to Greener Pastures any time you want to get him out of your hair?"

"That's right. I just need him off my premises for a few hours each day." Jade's eyes were taking on a feverish sheen. I hated to be the one to burst her bubble.

"But how will that get him out of your hair? With one trip I can supply you with enough sap to more than meet your needs."

"He doesn't know that though, does he? I'll send him every day for a bit at a time. He won't know any better if I tell him the sap has to be harvested fresh daily to make the best wine."

"I'll agree under one condition."

"I'm desperate enough to agree to almost anything."

"We sit down and calmly discuss how much sap each of us needs for our businesses and how much there is available."

"Okay. Done."

"Not quite. You are going to have to put in some time

in the sugar bush learning what goes into making the sap ready for Knowlton to pick up."

"Agreed."

"I'm still not done. I also want to pick your brain for some tips for the sugarhouse retail shop and I want to brainstorm some crossover marketing between our two businesses."

"That's a great idea. I can just see it all now. Gift baskets, tastings at both shops, really highlighting the close-knit family angle." Jade jumped up off the couch and grabbed her jacket. "I'm going to go home and get thinking about this right away." Before I could say another word she was gone, leaving her basket of goodies on the table.

I helped myself to another cracker with chutney and wondered about how in the world the problem of Knowlton could possibly have set my relationship with Jade on a new and better path.

Twenty-five

Even though I hadn't wanted to provoke unwanted attention from Mitch I decided I'd better risk talking to his father. I found Gary up in the opera house, tinkering with a radiator. He looked up when he saw me and I wasn't sure if his frown was for me personally or if he wasn't happy to be interrupted.

"What brings you by, Dani? I would have thought you'd be out straight with the sugaring at this time of year." Gary pawed through his toolbox and lifted out an adjustable wrench.

"I have been busy but you know how much of a priority the opera house restoration is to the family. I felt like I had to make time to ask how things were going with the furnace upgrade."

"This mess sure has managed to make that job bigger." Gary gestured up at the ceiling. As positive as the impact of temperature changes is on sap in my maple trees, water in pipes has a whole different attitude to below-freezing temperatures.

Just as the sugaring season was set to begin the pipes in the opera house portion of the town hall building had frozen and burst. Water had started streaming into the plaster walls of the opera house and down into the ceiling of the floors below.

Pipes all over town had frozen and every decent repairperson had worked almost around the clock. Gary had been working nonstop himself for a couple of weeks. Since the opera house wasn't being used while the renovations were being done we had agreed that he should prioritize repairs in townspeople's homes.

The plaster ceilings that had been damaged were a thing of beauty before the water got to them. Flowers and vines and stars wrapped around light fixtures and traced the openings of the stairways. It was a glorious old building and it broke my heart to see it damaged so badly.

"I don't know what's going to be able to be done about the ceilings but if anyone can get the pipes straightened out I'm sure it's you." I wasn't just sweet-talking Gary to soften him up. He was great at his job. People had trusted their plumbing and heating systems to him for years. Almost exactly as many years as it had been since Spooner disappeared. "After all, you've been tending to this heating system for years, haven't you?"

"I was an apprentice when the last system went in at the town hall. That was a big job, too, but at least the plaster wasn't affected that time."

"So you must have gone into the business just about the time you and Theresa were thinking about getting married."

"That's right. I wanted to have a steady job with decent pay if I was going to have a family, and my father gave me some good advice. He said there wasn't ever going to be a lack of need for furnaces in New Hampshire and that pipes always managed to get themselves frozen."

"Sounds like a smart guy."

"About some things he was. I liked working with my hands and my mother's brother owned a plumbing and heating business."

"That was lucky."

"It was. I started working as a part-time grunt work guy during the summers when I was in high school. When I graduated my uncle hired me on full-time and I started learning the trade in earnest."

"How long was it before you went into business for yourself?"

"Years. I worked for my uncle well into my thirties and then he decided to retire and I bought his business from him. I was hoping Mitch would want to follow in my footsteps but he was more interested in joining the police force." Gary shook his head and tossed the wrench back into his toolbox with a clang.

"If it helps, I wish he hadn't decided to be a cop either." With Mitch's general interest in ticketing me for everything from jaywalking to breathing too loudly I would have much preferred him to work in the plumbing and heating industry.

"I was always sorry things didn't work out for the two of you but you can't pick a spouse for your kids any more than you can choose a job for them."

"I think it's best when the people most involved are left to their own devices. Look at you and Theresa for example. The two of you have been happily married forever and I understood you were high school sweethearts. I don't expect your families orchestrated that."

"Nope. I'd known Theresa practically all my life but it wasn't until third-period geometry class that I really noticed her. I almost flunked the course from spending so much time trying to get her attention instead of paying attention to the teacher."

"Theresa told me you got married only a few months after she graduated from high school."

"We did. I had proposed while she was in her senior year and she had accepted but wasn't wearing the ring because she didn't want her mother to know how serious things had gotten. Her mother was very protective of Theresa and her reputation."

"I've heard you were pretty protective of her, too." I held my breath and hoped Gary wasn't going to be offended and stop talking.

"Sounds like you've heard about Spooner Duffy." Gary stood up and crossed his arms over his chest. Mitch had gotten his height from his father. I could feel the way Gary was looming over me and the thought crossed my mind that asking him irritating questions without a witness might have been a bad idea.

"His body being found has brought up a lot of old memories."

"And old gossip. I suppose people are saying I had a key to the town hall and was angry about the way Spooner kept chasing Theresa."

"It has been mentioned."

"Are you the one doing the mentioning?"

"No. I'm just trying to get the restoration job back under way so I can focus on my sugaring."

"Then I suggest you stop distracting me with old nonsense and let me get back to work on the task at hand." Gary started to turn his back on me like he was done talking. I figured there was little to lose in aggravating him further so I decided to push my luck.

"Does that mean you didn't kill Spooner and bury him under a pile of coal in the basement?"

"It means that even if I did I wouldn't have time to tell you about it and to repair the plumbing. If you keep pestering me and insulting me I might just decide I'm too busy to work on this job at all." With that he pointed to the door.

If I wanted to be able to question Frances about her finances or any knowledge she might have had concerning Spooner's unfortunate demise, I had to get her to agree to see me once more. After the disastrous end to our last meeting I needed something quite convincing to get her to allow me back into her apartment. Fortunately, I knew just the thing.

My apartment door was only one of two at the top of the stairs leading up from the back room at Stems and Hems. The other led to a storage area where Frances had left her scrapbooks and other bulky items she still valued but had no room for at Dappled Oaks. If I appeared at her door carrying the albums she had mentioned wanting returned I doubted she would refuse to see me. It was just as possible she wouldn't remember she had been angry with me in the first place.

I tried the knob on the storage room and even though it squeaked, it turned. The door swung open easily. I stepped inside and was able to imagine how my apartment would have looked before the interior walls had been added. Sloping attic ceilings brought nails protruding roughly through to the roof to secure the shingles so low they nearly scraped my head.

Unlike my apartment this space had no dormers and only very small windows cut into the gable end. I made my way through stacks and stacks of boxes and finally found a few with Frances's name written on the outside in bold black letters. I found the albums in the second one I opened.

I clutched the albums tightly to my chest as I picked my way back through the gloom. It wouldn't endear me to Frances if I damaged something that meant so much to her. Back in the apartment I wrapped the albums in plastic shopping bags and then slid them into a sturdy canvas tote bag. After grabbing a snack and running a brush through my hair I was ready to head off to visit Frances once more.

I checked in at Dappled Oaks' front desk and made my way to Frances's apartment. I had barely landed a blow on the door when she yanked it open as wide as the chain would allow. The thought crossed my mind that she was paranoid enough that she stood all day with her eye pressed to the peephole, keeping a watch on the hallway.

"I'm not buying any of your Squirrel Squad taffy. I just had a crown repaired," Frances said through the narrow opening. Well, at least she remembered me enough to link me with my Squirrel Squad fund-raising days. I'd like to think I looked older than I had in my gray uniform but the truth was, I probably didn't.

"I haven't come about the squirrels. I've brought you your albums from the storage area at Stems and Hems." I pulled one out and carefully unwrapped it before holding it up for her to see. She pressed her face against the crack and I saw her eye widen in recognition. A second later I heard the chain sliding in its track and Frances's hand clutched my arm and dragged me inside.

"Where did you say you found these?" Frances sat at the little table in the kitchenette and held out her hands for the albums. I placed them gently, one at a time, in front of her. She opened a photo album first and peered at the faces smiling up at her from the pages.

"In the storage area above Stems and Hems. Right where you told me they'd be. They were in a storage box."

"My memory isn't what it used to be, you know," Frances said, turning the pages of her album. "But when

I look at these photos I remember the things in them like it was yesterday." I sat next to her and looked at the photo she was pointing at.

"Are these members of your family?" I asked.

"They are. This whole album is of my parents and cousins and even aunts and grandparents. All of them gone now. There's just me left." Frances looked around the apartment and for a moment I thought she would cry. Then she turned to the other album. "This one is of other people and events." She closed her family album and pulled the one filled with friends toward her.

"Does it include any photos of the maple festival?" I asked.

"Most of the photos were of the festival. It was my favorite event every year. And the scrapbook is full of memorabilia like programs and ticket stubs. I even made notes about the weather and jotted down things that went well or things we'd want to do differently the next year."

"What a great idea. Would you show me? I might want to try something like that myself since I'm on the festival committee now."

"Of course. Here is an entry from 1968. Look at all the men in their hats. I always think a man in a hat looks so dapper. Don't you?" Frances traced her finger over a photo of a group of men. I leaned in for a better look and recognized my grandfather and Doc. Both smiled out at the camera, their faces not so lined as they were now.

"They certainly do look distinguished. How many years does the scrapbook cover?"

"I added to it for a long time. See." Frances flipped through the album and stopped three-quarters of the way through. "This is the year Theresa won the Miss Maple pageant. I had just started training her at the bank about a week or so before the festival."

"She looks so happy," I said. The photo of Theresa showed a beautiful young woman with a dazzling smile. It was easy to see why as a young pageant contestant Jade had idolized her and had wanted to follow in her footsteps.

"She was. She worked so hard on her talent even practicing during her lunch break at the bank to be ready."

"What was her talent?" I never had thought to ask. Jade's obsession with the pageant had kind of turned me off to the whole thing.

"She did an escape artist routine where she had to pick the lock on a set of handcuffs and get out of a wooden cabinet blindfolded. The judges loved it."

"I'll bet they did." It was funny Theresa hadn't mentioned her ability to pick locks as one of the reasons Preston suspected her in the theft. After all, Karen's desk drawer lock had been picked.

Frances leafed a few pages ahead. "And here is the last one of that year. I took it of Tansey, Jim, and Spooner after the festival ended and we were collecting up the earnings."

I looked closely at that one. It was my first look at Spooner, well at least at more than a few bits of his bones. He was the spitting image of Knowlton and I wondered how Tansey ever thought she had kept his parentage a secret from anyone who remembered Spooner.

Even in the photo it was easy to see Tansey wasn't well. Jim looked like himself only without the slight paunch he now had and with a full head of hair that he didn't possess anymore.

"Spooner was with you when you were handling the money raised from the festival?"

"He was an enormous help that year. I don't know what we would have done without him."

"What kind of things did he do for you?"

"A little of everything. He hung signs and manned one of the parking lots. He did a lot of work setting up the booths along Main Street in the days leading up to the event. He even offered to take the money to the town hall since he was heading there anyway." Frances turned the page and started to talk about the next year when I stopped her.

"Spooner was the one who was in charge of taking the money to the town hall?" This was the first I had heard of that. Even Preston and Lowell hadn't said anything about it. And, strangely enough, neither had Tansey. "Are you certain about that?" I tried to keep the excitement out of my voice but I don't think I managed to.

"Oh dear, I think I wasn't supposed to tell anyone that." Frances snapped the album shut and shoved back her chair.

"Why weren't you supposed to tell anyone? Was it because that was the year the money went missing?"

"I knew you were a spy. I want you to go." It looked like our visit was over. Without another word Frances grabbed me by the arm and pulled me to the door. "And I don't want you to come back." With that, she shoved me out and slammed the door shut behind me. If I wanted answers it was clear I was going to have to ask someone else.

I decided to ask Jim for confirmation of Frances's story about Spooner and the deposit money. After all, Frances wasn't the most reliable source of information. And he seemed like an easier person to talk to about it than Tansey. She'd been through a lot already and if Frances was just misremembering the details, there was no reason to upset her about anything else.

Twenty-six

 "Some new information has come to light about who handled the bank deposit. Do you want to change your story?" I asked.

"It was supposed to be Tansey and me." Jim sat behind his desk at the real estate office.

"Supposed to be? Did the two of you end up taking it or not?"

"No. At the last minute Tansey wasn't feeling well and asked if someone could drive her home instead. And I met a couple at the festival who were so enchanted with Sugar Grove they wanted to view some property before they headed back out of state. I couldn't turn them down. Spooner said he still needed to go to the town hall to work on the painting job. He offered to take the money for us if someone else took Tansey home and left him with Tansey's truck."

"So did you take him up on the offer?"

"We did. We never thought anything of it. He had been such a help and it made sense to have him take it since he was going there anyway. Besides, it was Sugar Grove, not some high-crime area. Frances offered to give Tansey a ride home and I was glad she did. I really needed the business and the couple looked like they had money to burn."

"But you decided to lie about who took the money once you realized it was missing?"

"We did. I called Tansey and Frances right away to get our stories straight. None of us liked lying but we thought it was the best thing to do under the circumstances."

"That must have been an uncomfortable position to be in."

"It would have been if Preston hadn't been so set on Spooner as the thief that he didn't really give anyone else a look. I kept waiting for him to question me about it and I had no idea if I could keep up the pretense."

"You must have been pretty worried."

"I was beside myself. If Preston figured out we were lying or if someone's conscience got the better of them, my reputation as an honest person to do business with would have been ruined."

"Is that why you made sure Preston knew about the affair his wife was having with Spooner, to distract him from thinking too much about anyone else?" Jim slumped in his chair and nodded.

"I'm not proud of what I did but I felt desperate at

the time. Preston's entire focus of the investigation remained on Spooner as soon as I'd opened my mouth about seeing Karen with Spooner at the town hall."

"You cost Karen not only her marriage but her job as the town clerk. A job she loved, by the way."

"What can I say? I was weak and frightened. But I made it up to Karen by helping her start up her property management business." Jim flashed me a salesman's smile. I was glad I had already rented Priscilla's apartment. If I hadn't before, there was no way I could have brought myself to do business with Jim.

"Karen hates being a property manager. And you do realize you helped a murderer go free for thirty years, don't you?" Jim just gave me a sad nod before I stomped back out his door.

I drove on out to Tansey's place and pulled right up next to the barn. Steam billowed out of the cupola, which told me she hadn't been able to resist sugaring no matter what she had said about giving up the business. Sugaring is a lot like farming. There is a rhythm to the seasons that gets into your bones and won't let you ignore it.

I don't know what would have to be happening in my life to keep me from sugaring. It would be like wasting a beautiful early summer day on television watching or shopping in a mall. Even if I did it I'd feel guilty and I'd never be able to enjoy it.

Tansey had her back to me when I entered the barn with her old dog following me. She was shoving a stick of wood into the firebox and didn't hear me until I was just behind her.

"You could give a body a heart attack sneaking up on someone like that," Tansey said. "Have you got some news for me?"

"More like some questions. I've been to see Frances."

"Good for you. I'm sure she could use the company. What's it got to do with me?"

"Why didn't you tell me Spooner took the money to the town hall the night he and it disappeared?" I tried to keep from sounding shrill but from the way Tansey's dog flattened his ears I'd say I hadn't managed it.

"I thought it would have been harder for you to keep an open mind about the possibility that he didn't steal the funds if you knew he'd handled the money. From your reaction I'd say I was right not to bring it up."

Tansey sank into one of the beat-up old lawn chairs she kept in the barn and pointed at the one next to her. I didn't want to sit around chatting with her. I'd already wasted too much time I didn't have to spare on what looked like a mystery that had already been solved.

"You've wasted my time and you know how little there is at this time of year."

"I know it looks bad but I still can't believe Spooner was responsible for taking the money."

"You still should have told me all that you knew."

"It seemed like the right decision at the time. Someday when you have children of your own you'll understand."

"That doesn't seem like much of an excuse."

"It was late and I was exhausted. If you ever get

pregnant you'll understand that, too. I'd never been so tired in my life as I was that day. And sick, too. Morning sick didn't begin to describe what I went through. I was sick every minute I was awake and even dreamt of being sick some nights." Tansey closed her eyes like she was traveling back in time in her mind. "And Jim had met a couple from out of state at the festival that wanted him to show them a house he had listed before they headed home that night. He was new in the business and eager to make a go of it so he agreed even though he had committed to taking the money to the town hall."

"That still doesn't explain everything."

"No one knew why I was sick and when they all assumed I was coming down with the flu I didn't correct their assumption. Spooner said he was planning to work through the night on the paint job he was doing at the town hall. I was supposed to pick him up in the morning since he didn't have his own vehicle."

"And?"

"So, everyone thought I was going to be sick and stuck in bed in the morning. So Spooner offered to take my truck and the money over to the town hall so he could drive himself back here when he was done and save me the trouble. We all agreed and Frances drove me home."

"And none of you said anything to Preston when the money and Spooner went missing?"

"Of course not. I didn't want to draw attention to my illness in case anyone was paying attention to my weight gain and weird food cravings. Jim didn't want to look like he wasn't capable of making good decisions. After all, a Realtor is in a position of trust in a community and it would have looked like we weren't worthy of that. It was bad enough as it was without us looking like a bunch of bumblers for being taken in by a thief."

"Why didn't Frances say anything?"

"Because she was a good sport and a good friend. I told her on the drive back to my place that I was pregnant and she didn't want to make things harder on me. I never told her who the father was though."

"So none of you were willing to tell Preston what had really happened?" I had always thought of Tansey as such a straight arrow. The idea that she was involved with lying to the police and impeding an ongoing investigation was shocking. It made me even more unsure about how much I could trust that she hadn't had something to do with Spooner's death.

"We didn't have any idea at the time that Spooner was dead and that someone else could have killed him in order to make off with the money. It just didn't seem important enough to jump up and down and point our fingers at ourselves. You must have heard of the way Preston lorded over everyone when he was the chief."

I had heard the stories of Preston's delight at flexing his investigative powers. He had a reputation for turning a squashed woodchuck in the middle of the highway into a hit-and-run homicide investigation. Tansey did have a point. But so did I.

"Tansey, do you realize that Spooner could have been killed just as much for the money as for any other reason?" Like his unstoppable pursuit of the women in town. "If you and Jim had dropped off the money Russ might have uncovered your bodies in the town hall instead." If Tansey hadn't been sitting I was sure she would have keeled right over. Her knees knocked together and the lawn chair shook like her barn sat on a fault line.

"But that would mean Knowlton never would have been born." Tansey's face paled even lighter than her usual shade of midwinter white. "Can you imagine that?"

I'm not proud of myself for saying so but I did think for a second how Knowlton not existing might have improved my life in many ways. Particularly my teen years.

"What I am imagining is that this means Lowell should be looking at people who might have known about Spooner carrying the money as much as he is people with animosity toward Spooner in particular. Do you know if anyone outside the festival committee overheard you talking to Spooner about carrying the money to the town hall?" It was a long shot after all these years but maybe Tansey would remember someone hanging around after the festival.

"There weren't many people just milling around. And we didn't exactly linger either. Different committee members were responsible for collecting money at different points at the end of the festival and putting it all together into one deposit bag. Unless one of us told someone else I can't imagine how anyone could have known."

Tansey had stopped shaking and looked thoughtful,

like she was casting her mind a long way back. "Besides, no one ever came forward to say that Spooner had been the one carrying the money. I think that goes to show no one knew."

"Or it goes to show that whoever did had a very good reason to keep quiet about it."

"You mean they didn't want to be a snitch?" Tansey nodded like she approved of people minding their own darn business.

"I mean, like that someone is the person who killed him."

Twenty-seven

I may have promised to help Tansey clear Spooner's name but that was before she had kept important information from me. As much as I didn't want her to drop out of the festival committee my greater loyalty lay with Lowell and with whatever would help solve Spooner's murder. I pulled into a spot at the police station and gave myself a moment to figure out what I wanted from the conversation.

Myra's desk chair was empty and her light was switched off, both signs she must be gone for the day. I heard muted voices coming from behind Lowell's closed office door and after having had an uncomfortable experience back at Thanksgiving I made sure to knock and wait for permission to enter. Lowell's voice boomed out and invited me in and I was not surprised to see my mother seated in the visitor chair.

"I hope I'm not interrupting anything," I said and found that I meant it. It had taken some time for me to get used to it but now it was clear to me my mother and Lowell's relationship made them both very happy. Accepting it and supporting them in it made me a lot happier than trying to make them feel guilty about it.

"You aren't the family member we're trying to avoid," Mom said. "Hazel has taken it upon herself to remind Lowell of how much she likes a man in uniform. We thought it best that he not visit the house any more than necessary until she leaves."

"He could avoid the house entirely, couldn't he?" I asked.

"I could if she would stop dialing 911 and making up fake emergencies."

"Why don't you tell her you'll arrest her for wasting police time?" I asked. Lowell's face flushed and he seemed to find something on the floor worth staring at.

"I did the third time I arrived at Greener Pastures to find she was not in the throes of a crisis."

"So why didn't it help?" Not that it would be easy to dissuade Hazel from any course of action she felt inclined to pursue.

"Lowell thought it best to beat a hasty retreat when she pointed out all the ways the two of them could enjoy using his handcuffs in the back of the cruiser," Mom said. "I told him he should have taken her up on the opportunity to learn a thing or two but he didn't like the suggestion."

"I took the cuffs straight home and wiped them down

with bleach but they still seem dirty to me." Lowell shook his head and I wondered if it would be against department regulations to purchase him a new pair as a gift.

"She's managed to drive Graham off for similar reasons. He still won't tell me all the details of their lunch together the day Russ found Spooner's body. Which is really why I'm here."

"Any news about the money coming to light as a result of your expert snooping?" Lowell asked.

"Not in the way Tansey had hoped but I did find out something that may point your investigation in a new direction," I said. "I stopped by to visit Frances Doucette and while we were looking over one of her scrapbooks she forgot she was supposed to keep something a secret."

"Something helpful, I hope," Lowell said.

"Spooner was the one who took the earnings from the festival to the town hall instead of Jim and Tansey like they'd claimed in the police report."

"By himself?" Lowell asked as he pulled a notebook and a pencil close and started to make notes.

"Yes. Tansey was sick and Jim had a showing crop up unexpectedly so Spooner offered to take the money to the town hall. Frances said he was planning on working on that paint job at the town hall that night anyway so they took him up on it."

"Have you asked Jim or Tansey for confirmation of this?"

"First I checked with Jim then went on to Tansey's. I came here directly from her place. They both admitted that Spooner was the one who was supposed to take the money to the town hall."

"But they didn't know if he ever actually got there with it?"

"No. No one seems to know that for sure."

"So his murder may have had more to do with someone taking advantage of him having the money than it did about him personally."

"That's what I was thinking."

"The investigation always should have focused more on whether or not someone had unusual amounts of money to spend after the theft. I told Preston that at the time." Lowell jabbed his pencil down on the desk, breaking it in half. It was rare for him to lose his temper and raise his voice. It was even more unexpected for him to show physical signs of his anger. The case must really have been frustrating him. "I don't want you looking into this anymore."

"Good, because I don't want to waste any more of my time on it either. I'm already angry at Tansey for keeping things from me and the least bit of discouragement from you is music to my ears."

"This is serious, Dani. If the person who killed Spooner did it for the money they aren't going to take too kindly to you trying to figure things out. I want you done with this as of this minute."

"I wasn't being flip. You know how busy I am with the sugaring and with the festival planning. Since Tansey couldn't be honest with me I'm done." I felt my shoulders roll back and a sense of calm descend on me.

"That is, I'll consider myself out of it as soon as I share with you what I learned about some unexplained money in town."

I waited while Lowell dug a fresh pencil out of his drawer and then told him about the prize money Doc had given Theresa and the unexpected contributions that had landed in the collection plate at the church.

"Not to tell you how to do your job but it seems to me the offering money might be the best lead. Even Grandpa didn't have any idea where it came from."

"Your father knows where it was from," Mom said. Lowell shot me as covert a look as he could but she caught him at it and sighed deeply. "After all the proof you've had of my connection to other realms I am surprised at your attitude. I'm not sure you're a very good influence on my daughter."

"I'm sorry, Kelly. What does Forrest have to say?" Lowell asked.

"The money came from book sales."

"Book sales?" Lowell and I repeated at the same time.

"He's very clear. Book sales." Mom paused and squinted like she was trying to make out the details of something off in the distance. "I'm sure of it."

"What exactly did Dad show you this time?" I was rewarded with a beaming smile. Mom loved it when someone wanted to talk paranormal stuff with her.

"He's showing me row after row of books, all sorts and conditions. A hand is lifting them up one by one and pulling out a dollar bill from each and throwing it up in the air."

"And you think that means someone sold used books and offered the money up to God?" It wasn't the kookiest theory she had come up with for what Dad was trying to say.

Even when he wrote out a list for her in black and white of things he needed from a store when he was alive, she would come back with aquarium fish instead of fish fillets or cashews instead of the nuts from the hardware store. Things hadn't really improved since he had passed over to the other side.

"Do you have a better suggestion?" Mom asked. She had me there. I was stumped. I wished, not for the first time, that Dad had learned to write his thoughts down clearly on poster board in the afterlife and then could hold them up for Mom to read. It would still be an otherworldly communication but it would just be so much more efficient. Unfortunately, there didn't seem to be any sort of customer service representative I could call about it.

"What about if someone found a whole lot of money tucked into some books and felt guilty about it so they gave it away? Especially since it didn't belong to them?" Lowell said.

"I think you're right," Mom said. She squinted even harder and nodded. "Forrest is nodding at me like you made a good suggestion."

"But does that have anything to do with the money from the festival being stolen? If it is from the sale of used books it can't be the stolen money." I had to ask. It wasn't that I didn't enjoy hearing from my father but if getting information from beyond the grave was going to be more useful than a party trick we needed to keep on point.

"I don't know. Dani, he's pointing at you and then covering his eyes."

"Like shielding them from the sun?" I asked.

"He's mouthing something while he has them covered."

"Could he be counting?" Lowell asked. "Like for hide-and-seek?"

"Exactly," Mom said. "He started nodding right up and down as soon as you said that. And now he's pointing at you again, Dani."

"What does that mean? Does he want to play hide-and-seek with me? Is it my turn to seek?" I asked.

"He's gone." Mom slumped back in her chair and dug in her bag for a mint. She seemed to need a hit of sugar right after her psychic experiences. Lowell looked more like he could use a stiff drink.

As much as his relationship with my mother still made me slightly uncomfortable I had to give Lowell high marks for being a stand-up guy. It couldn't be easy dating your best friend's widow. It would be even harder if your dead friend kept getting in touch with the two of you.

"None of this has any bearing on what I said, Dani. I want you to get back to the business of sugaring and planning the festival," Lowell said. "Leave the investigating to me. I'll speak to Tansey myself and tell her you're done on my say-so."

Twenty-eight

Mountain View Food Mart was a madhouse when I stopped to pick up some food. With a storm moving in, the place was packed. If I were still at Greener Pastures I could have avoided the grocer during such a peak time. Grandma's pantry was so well stocked Grandpa joked we could withstand a six-month siege if need be.

But my supplies included a half a bag of butterscotch disks and a couple of plastic containers of leftovers Grandma had sent with me because she worried I would starve. I didn't even have enough toilet paper to last me until the morning.

I waved hello to Myra and managed to avoid Knowlton's eye as I added more and more items to my cart. I bumped into Theresa at the cantaloupe display where she was sniffing each melon in turn, looking for a ripe one.

"Hey, Dani, seeing you reminds me I've been racking

my brain about something to do with the festival and the banking. Something odd but I can't quite remember what it was. Something about the stopped payment on the checks." Theresa shook her head as she put a melon in her cart.

"What kind of a something?"

"It feels like a negative thing. Like instead of something being where it shouldn't be that something was missing where it should be instead. If I think of it I'll give you a call." Theresa moved on to the display of bananas and left me feeling restless.

I pushed my cart toward the bread aisle, took one look at the carnage, and decided I would stock up on pasta instead. Ten minutes later I was in the parking lot loading the groceries into the back of the family minivan when Knowlton appeared next to me.

"Want some help?" he asked. As much as getting out of interactions with Knowlton is my usual mode of operating, I noticed the snowflakes had turned from large friendly ones to those small mean ones that indicate you'd best get under cover and stay there. The forecast had been calling for twelve to eighteen inches and with the two that had built up on the ground since I had left for Dappled Oaks earlier, I could believe it. I'd be smart to take him up on his offer.

"Thanks, Knowlton. You look better." I felt good saying so because he *did* look better than he had the last few times I'd seen him. He had remembered to wear a coat and he stood up straight instead of stooped over like an old man.

"That's because Mother's doing a lot better than she was. She actually drove over to the post office today," he said as he piled a bag holding a gallon of milk onto my carton of eggs.

"I'm glad to hear it. What do you think is the reason for the improvement in her spirits?"

"She's started planning my wedding," Knowlton said. My muscles all tensed and my body went rigid. If a stiff wind blew me over I knew I would shatter into thousands of little pieces and the street-sweeping machine would wipe me up in the spring. "Of course, Jade hasn't said yes yet but Mother is hopeful. I've been spending every spare minute over at the winery proving to Jade how good we are together."

"I noticed you haven't been at Greener Pastures as much as usual." Knowlton looked sheepishly at his feet then tossed a twelve-pack of toilet paper on top of a rosemary plant I had picked up to brighten my windowsill.

"I feel kind of bad about turning my back on you as soon as Jade came to town but I can't deny my true feelings."

"I wouldn't expect you to."

"Jade is the girl for me and as long as she's in Sugar Grove I consider myself to be her devoted love slave."

An image of Knowlton dressed in not much more than a metal-studded dog collar flashed through my mind. Between the relief that he was dumping me for Jade and the trauma of the pictures in my mind I felt like I was suffering emotional whiplash. I also thought about what Jade must be going through with her new business, her worries about Hazel, and life in general. It occurred to me I might do my cousin a good turn.

"You've got to follow your heart. And to show I've got no hard feelings I'd like to give you a piece of advice about Jade."

"I'm all ears." In Knowlton's case this was almost true. He did have a prizewinning set of head ornaments. Long, wide, and set onto his head at an angle that made his head look almost as broad as his shoulders, Knowlton's ears were one of his most memorable features.

"Jade likes what is rare. She likes things that are not so easy to obtain. I think the right strategy with her is to play a little hard to get."

"Are you sure you're not just trying to get me to leave her alone?"

"I moved out of Greener Pastures as soon as Jade moved in. How likely do you think it is that I would try to help her out?" It wasn't a lie. Not exactly. Knowlton knew our history. How he determined it would influence my actions was his own business.

"Dani, I think it's sweet that you would stoop so low to try to ensnare my affections once more. Jade's my one true love and nothing is going to change my mind." He stepped away from the back of the minivan just as I put the last bag into it. "I think it would be best if we didn't see much of each other for a while. You need some time to get me out of your system." He turned his back on me and slipped off through the storm, leaving me to try to reach the minivan's tailgate all on my own.

Twenty-nine

Snow was falling hard and fast by the time I slid to a stop in the parking space behind Stems and Hems. Priscilla's car was still there and covered with at least three inches of snow. I wondered if anyone was likely to come into the shop to buy flowers during a storm but Priscilla was conscientious.

I'd never heard of her closing early for weather in the past. I hoped she'd be safe on her drive over to her lake-front house. It was a few miles out of town and the roads by the lake were mostly private and poorly maintained.

I'd been white-knuckling the wheel for the entire drive and was relieved when it was over even though my own trip was less than two miles. Sleet was mixing in with the snow and the town crews couldn't get the roads salted and sanded fast enough to keep the roads easily passable. I sent up a good thought for the guys on the crew and added an item to my mental to-do list. In the morning I would take jugs of maple syrup over to the town barn to say thanks.

I noticed lights on in the first floor of the building and decided Priscilla really hadn't closed early. Better her than me, I thought as I climbed the stairs to the second floor and pushed open the door to the apartment. The apartment felt warm compared to the outdoors but I still felt damp and chilly.

I changed into some cozy pajama pants and a ratty fleece sweatshirt with a hood. After rounding up a flashlight, some candles and matches, and filling buckets with water in case the power went out I fixed myself a mug of chai and sweetened it with a dollop of maple syrup.

By the time the tea was cool enough to sip I'd settled myself on the comfy love seat with a quilt and a book. The wind howled outside and the sleet pinged against the windowpanes but I was safe and dry and grateful that as nasty as the weather was it was worse in the book I was reading.

It was strange to be so alone, to have no noises of the family filtering through the walls or up the stairs. It felt odd that no one was going to knock on the door and ask if I wanted to play a board game or to offer me a bowl of popcorn. But, no one was going to remind me it was my turn with the dishes either. I could surrender myself entirely to the story and that felt luxurious.

I was not pleased when only a few minutes later my phone rang. I thought seriously about not answering it.

After all, Lowell had said it was time to leave the investigating to him. Theresa's name on the screen was sure to mean she was calling about something to do with that instead of a personal call. I couldn't just let it go to voice mail though. I never can ignore a ringing phone.

I closed the Icelandic crime novel I had been reading and promised myself I'd keep the call short.

"I've been racking my brain and I finally thought of what I was trying to remember about the stopped checks," Theresa said. I should have stopped her right there and told her to call Lowell. But it seemed like it would be faster to just hear her out and then report any information to Lowell myself later. I would get back to reading about the wilds of Scandinavia faster that way.

"I'm all ears."

"It was Frances. For about a month after the festival money was stolen she would ask me every day when she got back from lunch if a certain someone had called or come in to put a stop payment on one of the checks that had gone missing."

"Who was she asking about?"

"Priscilla. Every day she asked me if Priscilla had put a stop payment on her raffle ticket check. Finally one day she didn't ask and I teased her about it a bit. I asked her why she didn't ask me and she said to forget about the whole thing."

"Did she seem upset?"

"She did, kinda. Frances was always nice to work with. A little fussy and just so about everything but then, that's a plus in the banking business. But when I teased her about her obsession with Priscilla's check she got really flustered and then very snippy. She cut me off and never mentioned it again."

I hung up with Theresa and opened my book. I snuggled deep under the quilt and focused my eyes on the pages in front of me. Unfortunately, I couldn't concentrate on the words. My mind kept returning to the conversation with Theresa. Why would Frances have been concerned with Priscilla's checking account? Priscilla was so careful with her record keeping I couldn't imagine there was really cause to worry.

But as I thought about it some more I considered Frances's habits, too. She might be having some trouble with being paranoid as she had grown older but she had always been a reasonable enough person earlier in her life. I didn't think she would fixate on something like Priscilla's check without a reason. After all, they had been friends for years and if she was worried for her there must have been a reason.

And even stranger, what had convinced her to stop asking about the check and why had she been so flustered about it when Theresa had inquired? Was it the teasing way Theresa had asked or was there another reason for her attitude?

I kicked off the quilt and wondered if I should go downstairs to ask Priscilla about the whole thing. But maybe she didn't know anything about it. After all,

Frances had been asking Theresa about it but there was no mention of her speaking to Priscilla directly.

I thought about phoning Frances but her memory was so sketchy and if she did remember the incident she likely wouldn't welcome questions from me on the subject. I considered calling Lowell but there wasn't much to tell. Technically he was off duty that evening but with the weather being as bad as it was he was likely to get called out to at least one accident.

And if the power went out, as it so often did when ice and heavy snow coated the power lines, he'd have his hands full without me adding to his problems. This information could wait until morning.

I tried checking my e-mail instead of reading and even thought about cooking something but still couldn't get the conversation out of my mind. Then, with a wave of relief, I remembered Frances had left more boxes in the storage room and Priscilla kept all her old tax records there.

I tugged on my heavy-duty fleece-lined suede slippers, grabbed the flashlight from the coffee table, and crossed the narrow hallway to the storage room door. I yanked it open with a loud squeak and picked my way across the splintery floorboards.

The heat from the store below pulsed up to me through the floorboards and the air was warmer than I had expected. In a few spots the floorboards were missing and I could see the underside of the ceiling tiles that served the shop below. The overhead light was weak but there was enough light to allow me to read the labeling on the storage boxes.

Besides the boxes with Frances's name on them there were many others labeled with dates. It was as though Priscilla had set things up to make snooping convenient. Even though the space was fairly warm I was glad the job might be an easy one. The wind whistled past and the building creaked and groaned. The light didn't shine back into the corners and I felt my imagination galloping off with me clinging to its back without a saddle. I turned on my flashlight and instantly felt braver.

In an effort to silence my curiosity I pried open the lid of the box marked with the year the festival money went missing. My stomach knotted up at the violation of trust I was committing. But I knew I couldn't just forget about it. I flicked through the musty file folders until I reached one labeled SUGAR GROVE CREDIT UNION.

Inside it I found a bundle of canceled checks barely held together by a dried-out rubber band. I slipped off the elastic and thumbed through the stack of checks. There was nothing to see that seemed to clear up my questions.

I returned the lid to the box and the box to the stack, hoping Priscilla wouldn't notice my fingermarks dragged through the dust. I eyed the labels on the rest of the boxes but none of the dates lined up with the year in question. I flicked my flashlight around the room and noticed a pair of filing cabinets at the gabled end.

I squeezed through the narrow passage between boxes and odd bits of furniture to the window where the filing cabinets sat silhouetted against the faint beam from the streetlight. I peered out the window at the storm.

Ice pellets skittered across the glass and the wind crept through unseen gaps between the frame and the panes. I shivered as the lights flickered. At Greener Pastures we had a generator as well as woodstoves, fireplaces, and Grampa's collection of oil lamps. I hadn't even thought to ask Priscilla if there was a generator for the store.

The responsible thing to do would be to leave off snooping and to trundle down the stairs to talk to Priscilla if she were still down in the shop. But there was no guarantee the power would go out and I was absolutely sure I wouldn't be able to settle back down with my book until I did all the poking around I could. I pulled open the top drawer of the nearest file cabinet with as little noise as possible.

The top three drawers contained nothing but warranty papers for old appliance purchases, vendor catalogs, and bridal and floral industry magazines. I knelt on the floor in front of the bottom drawer and pointed the flashlight into its depths. In the front of the drawer I found two shoe boxes full of photographic slides. I held a few up to the light and decided they were photos of wedding flowers and also before-and-after photos of Stems and Hems. I tucked the slides back into their boxes and squinted into the far reaches of the drawer. A bulging file marked MISCELLANEOUS took up most of the back of the drawer.

As I slid the file forward a zipper caught my eye. My heart thudded loudly in my chest as I realized what I was seeing. I reached into the folder and lifted out a bag. A Sugar Grove Credit Union bank bag. I tucked the flashlight under my arm with a trembling hand and pulled on the zipper. I wasn't sure if it was the age of the bag or the shaking of my hands but opening it proved to be harder than I would have expected.

I gave it a firmer tug and felt it budge. Little by little I eased the bag open. I adjusted the flashlight so it pointed into the bag and began rifling the contents. It was stuffed, simply stuffed, full of checks. I held my breath as I read them over and realized they were all made out to the Sugar Grove Maple Festival. And they were all dated for the weekend the money went missing. There was one last thing I wanted to know before I called Lowell.

I pulled the checks out and began to carefully inspect to whom they belonged. After I'd searched a stack at least an inch high I found what I was looking for but hoping not to find. Staring at me was a check written by Priscilla to the Sugar Grove Maple Festival. The reason Priscilla had not bothered to put a stop payment on her missing check was because she was the one who stole it.

Thirty

I slipped the checks back into the bag and rose to my feet. I needed to get back to my apartment to call Lowell. As I turned to leave a gasp caught in my throat.

"What do you think you're doing in here?" Priscilla stood a few steps into the room, blocking the doorway.

"I was just looking for some more albums Frances asked me to bring over to her," I said, hoping Priscilla hadn't noticed the bank bag in my hand.

"That isn't an album in your hand, now is it?" Priscilla took a few steps toward me and I was shocked to see a knife she used for trimming flowers in the shop in her hand.

"Well, no. It's not. You must have noticed how duffer-headed Frances is getting. Really quite paranoid, in fact.

She kept going on and on about people stealing her things, including stuff from her workdays. I decided to bring her this since I thought it might help ease her mind." I held my breath and hoped she'd buy it.

"You're lying." Priscilla took a few more steps toward me and pointed the knife at me.

"Why would I lie to you?" I looked around the room for a way to escape. Priscilla seemed to have as much trouble letting furniture and old clothes go as she did tax records and catalogs. All around me sat piles of coats, lamps with broken shades, and sagging mattresses.

"Because you know that bag wasn't with Frances's things and you know how it got there, don't you? Do you think I couldn't hear you moving boxes and opening the filing cabinets up here? The floor is so old and thin I could hear every twitch you made."

"I think this is the sort of thing we should talk about downstairs. It is dangerous up here and I don't know about you but I'm getting pretty cold." I didn't like the look in Priscilla's eyes. She was breathing pretty fast, too.

"I knew I should have gotten rid of that bank bag years ago." Priscilla's shoulders slumped a little, like she was ashamed of herself for not being able to let things go. The lights flickered again and I thought about whether my chances of getting past her were increased or decreased if the lights went out and stayed out. I hadn't noticed Priscilla carrying a flashlight of her own. I switched my flashlight off and slipped it into my sweatshirt pocket.

"Why didn't you?"

"Tax records. I just can't get rid of anything to do with them. I got audited early on in business and I have kept every scrap of paper ever since."

"You've got everything really well organized, too." Praise seemed like a good thing to try. "I bet you had a hard time deciding where to file the bank bag. Your system is so well designed it must have been difficult to settle on Miscellaneous." I edged a little closer to a wingback chair with a spring poking up through the fabric of the seat.

"You're right. I wanted to put it with the canceled checks but the checks weren't actually canceled."

"And most of them weren't yours. That must have been a factor, too." Perhaps appealing to her obsessive organizational skills wasn't the best choice but it was distracting her from the knife in her hand. If I could do it long enough I might get close enough to the door to make a break for it.

"You don't know how much trouble those things gave me or how many times I wished I hadn't kept them."

"I understand all the tidiness but what I don't get is how you ended up with them in the first place." It was obvious I wasn't fooling her into believing I thought the checks belonged to Frances. If I was going to be stabbed at least I could hear the whole story.

"You know if I tell you then you aren't going to be going anywhere, don't you?" Priscilla flashed the knife at me again. "I'll see to that."

"Even if you don't tell me it doesn't look like you are intending to let me leave," I said. "Besides, thirty years is a long time to lug around that sort of a secret. I bet you'd feel better if you finally told somebody about it. Maybe over a nice cup of tea in my apartment?"

"No tea, and you're right about me not letting you leave here no matter what." Priscilla pursed her lips. "But you're also right that it might do me some good to talk about it."

"You have such a successful business here. I can't see why you would have needed the money."

"It wasn't about me needing the money. It was about keeping it from someone else." Priscilla stepped even closer. At this rate she would be right on top of me before long. I took another step of my own toward the chair, hoping it would work as an effective shield if I should need it.

"But I thought the money was for a good cause?"

"If by a good cause you mean letting the cheapskate taxpayers in Sugar Grove get away with skimping on funding the library then I guess you could say that."

"How does stealing money slated for renovating the library help anyone?" I was worried by how animated and strident Priscilla's voice had become. It seemed like asking her about the money was not such a good idea after all. Instead of delaying her I had worked her up even more.

"The festival money would have been enough to fund nothing more than a pathetic redecorating project. And worse, one that the townspeople would have been able to claim met the community's needs for years to come. I was the only one willing to say we needed to raise a bond for a new separate building." That's when I remembered the message from my father about money blowing away from lots of books.

"So you decided to steal the money so the less costly project couldn't be done?"

"That's right. Frances had told me that the money was being kept overnight in Karen's desk drawer. So, I waited for a couple of hours after the festival was over and then let myself into the town hall with my keys."

"You had keys to the town hall?" Keys and who has them has always been a pretty lax affair in Sugar Grove. Even now in an era of car alarms and video surveillance most people still don't lock their doors.

"All the library trustees had keys to the town hall so we could get into the library when we needed to." Priscilla's face had taken on a smug look.

"So you let yourself in, but how did you manage to get the bank bag?"

"The cheap locks on those office desks are a joke. Anyone with a sturdy paper clip and a few minutes of free time can do it. I grabbed the bag and had headed around the corner to go downstairs when I ran right into Spooner."

"I bet that was a nasty surprise." Probably just about as nasty as being discovered snooping through a killer's incriminating papers in a dimly lit attic during a snowstorm. I almost felt bad for her.

"It all happened so fast. I spotted him. He spotted me and then pointed at the bank bag with a look of total surprise on his face."

"Did he say anything?"

"He said, 'Hey, what are you doing with that?' I was so startled I reached out both hands and shoved him."

"Did he fall down the stairs?"

"All the way down the whole flight. I had dropped the bank bag when I pushed him and it tumbled down the stairs with him. I was so shocked by what I had done I just stood there looking at him for a moment. His neck was twisted at a bizarre angle."

"Did you try to help him?"

"I snapped out of it and ran down to check his pulse but there wasn't one. I don't think he suffered much. I never meant to hurt him. All I wanted to do was to help the library. I even put the cash into the church collection plate a little at a time."

"How did his body get into the basement?"

"It was the only place to hide his body that I could think of. I grabbed him by the feet and hauled him bumpity bump down the basement stairs and left him there while I got my emergency snow shovel out of the trunk of my car."

"So you buried him in the basement all by yourself?"

"Of course I did. That's not the sort of thing you call the neighbors to give a hand with, now is it?" Priscilla had a point and thirty years earlier she would have been in her prime, physically, at least. "As much as the cheap slacker attitude in town was hard to take as far as getting a new library built, it helped me out with the body.

If the town elders hadn't been so lax about disposing of the coal in the basement it would have been a lot harder to hide the fact I had been digging around down there. As it was, I just dug as close as I could to the leftover pile and then tumbled coal from the pile down onto the grave."

"And no one was the wiser for thirty years."

"Not until you had to clean out the basement at the town hall. If it weren't for you Spooner would still be missing."

With that Priscilla lunged at me. I remembered what my father had supposedly said and looked for someplace that reminded me of hide-and-seek. The chair was all I had available. I crouched behind it just in time to feel Priscilla jabbing at the upholstery.

I heard a ripping sound over the howl of the wind and realized she was stabbing the chair with the knife. I was torn between wanting to keep a firm hold on the chair in order to use it as a shield and letting go of it in case she managed to hack all the way through. Before I could decide what to do I felt the chair begin to slide. Priscilla was pushing the whole thing in my direction.

The light was even lower under the eaves and I couldn't see what was behind me. Even with my small stature it only took a step backward before my head was scraping against the nails that held the shingles in place. I cried out as one gouged deeply into my scalp. The bank bag slipped from my grasp and fell to the floor.

I was pinned. Furniture stacked on either side of me

and the only way away from the nails in the ceiling was to move forward, straight into Priscilla. I tried to shove the chair back toward her to free myself. Priscilla had to have outweighed me by at least thirty pounds. I felt her use the full weight of her body against the chair. I did the only thing I could do. I let go of the chair and dropped to all fours, tucking myself into the gap under the eaves.

The chair slammed against the slope of the roof and stopped short. I pressed my face against the floor in an effort to keep Priscilla in my sights by peeking through the chair legs. For a second everything was dark and then there was a strange tearing noise. I heard Priscilla gasp with surprise as she took a final step forward and then a bit of light filtered up through the floorboards.

Everything happened so fast I thought I had imagined it. It took me a few seconds to convince myself I hadn't. From my hiding spot behind the chair I watched Priscilla drop through the floor right in front of me like she was riding an invisible elevator. First her calves disappeared from sight, then her torso, and finally her face with its look of complete surprise.

It was the thud that convinced me to leave my hiding spot. I looked around for the flashlight I had lost in the struggle but my sweating palms and trembling limbs made that job more difficult. I finally noticed the weight of it in my pocket. I pulled it out and switched it on. I crept along the floor joists, hoping they were more stable than whatever parts of the floor Priscilla had fallen through. I rounded the chair and crouched at the side of the hole.

I pointed the beam from my flashlight through the gap in the floor. The first thing it landed on was Priscilla's antique sewing machine. The second was Priscilla. She was slumped, motionless, on the floor, leaning against the base of the sewing machine.

Thirty-one

Somehow I found my way to the door and ignoring the quaking in my legs I hurried to Priscilla's side. Low security lighting gave off enough illumination to find her still slumped in the same position against the sewing machine's antique wooden base. I bent over her and tried to remember how to feel for a pulse.

I fumbled under the sleeve of her sweater, searching for the underside of her wrist. While I didn't think a medical school, or even an ambulance crew, was going to be knocking my door down any time soon with invitations to join them, I did manage to feel enough of a flickering throb to know Priscilla was still alive.

I stood and wandered the room, holding up my cell phone to look for coverage. The signal was faint but even over the crackling in and out I could make out Myra's voice. I shouted to make her understand to send the ambulance and Lowell to Stems and Hems. I turned on a few overhead lights. Then I returned to Priscilla's side and sat on the floor next to her. She still hadn't even twitched by the time Bob Sterling and Cliff Thompson rushed in with a stretcher.

Lowell was hot on their heels. He took one look at me and wrapped me in a snow-covered embrace. I was so relieved to feel safe I didn't even mind the snow melting off the brim of his uniform hat and landing on my head. As soon as Bob and Cliff had attended to Priscilla and were rushing her off to the hospital as fast as the storm would allow Lowell steered me over to the seating area Priscilla used for wedding consultations.

Lowell sat taking notes and only occasionally interrupting until I had told him everything.

"When she shoved the chair forward she must have uncovered a spot where there was nothing but lath and plaster. She punched straight through and hit her head on the cast-iron sewing machine when she fell."

"You were only supposed to be looking into the money and I told you to stop that part. You need someone keeping an eye on you twenty-four/seven." Lowell scowled at me and shook his head. "I don't think you ought to stay here on your own tonight." We both turned our heads toward the sound of heavy footsteps crossing the shop.

"My thoughts exactly." Graham hurried to my side and squatted next to my chair. "I came as soon as I heard this address on the radio. You okay?"

"She will be once she gets upstairs, has a hot shower, and some kind of sustaining beverage."

"Does that sound about right to you, Dani?" Graham asked. That was one of the things I really liked about him. He never acted like I didn't know my own mind.

"It sounds perfect. Lowell, please don't worry the family with any of this tonight. They'll feel like they need to rush over here to check on me and I don't want them out in the storm for no reason."

"Sure thing. As soon as the roads are clear in the morning I'd like you to come by the station to make a statement."

"Of course. But you'll want to take this with you now though." I picked up the bank bag and handed it to him. Lowell took it and gave me a peck on the top of my head. Graham and I walked him to the door and I led the way up the stairs to my apartment.

If I hadn't seen Priscilla leaving on a stretcher I would have been jumpy. As it was, with Graham's large, warm hand squeezing mine I just about managed to face the second floor once more.

After soothing myself in a long, hot shower I sat back on the sofa and pulled the quilt up over my body. Graham headed for the tiny kitchen and I could hear him filling a kettle with water. Before long he placed two steaming mugs on the trunk in front of the sofa. He sat next to me and lifted my feet into his lap, tucking the quilt around them. I felt all the tension of the last hour seeping from my body. Even with all that had happened just across the hallway it occurred to me there was no place I'd rather be.

"Do you want to talk about it?" Graham asked. "Or would you rather just sit quietly and listen to the storm?"

"I'm afraid I'm all talked out." I pulled my hand out from under the quilt and reached over to grasp his.

"Am I crowding you? You seem a little scrunched up. Would you rather I moved?" Graham asked. It occurred to me that something had changed. A few weeks ago my first thought after experiencing anything stressful would have been to head for Greener Pastures and the comfort of my family. Tonight, my first thought was that Graham was exactly the person I wanted to see coming through the door to comfort me.

"I think I'd be happier if we both moved." I kicked off the quilt and stood. I was most of the way to the bedroom before I looked back. Graham just stood there. My heart lurched and I wondered if I had embarrassed myself. "Aren't you interested?"

"I've been interested since the night you called in a mountain lion spotting. I just don't want to take advantage of someone still suffering from shock. Reaching out is a normal reaction to a near brush with death. I'd like this to be about more than that."

"You're right that what happened tonight has played a part in my invitation but not in the way you are suggesting."

"What do you mean?" Graham took a couple of steps closer to me.

"I mean, an experience like that clarifies priorities and makes you think about roads not yet taken. It made me certain this is a road I want to travel with you." I held out my hand. Graham reached forward to take it.

"Wait a minute," he said. "There's something important I need to know first."

"Okay," I said, a stampede of thoughts running through my head. "I'm listening."

"I'm not the sort of guy who shares a bed with a woman whose name I don't know." Graham pulled me close and bent toward my ear. "So before things go any further, you'll have to tell me, what's Dani short for?" Of all the thoughts I'd had, that was not one I'd considered.

"You promise not to laugh?" I asked. "Because that is guaranteed to kill the mood."

"My mother named me after a cracker. I'm in no position to poke fun at anyone else." Graham made a cross over his heart with his fingers. "I promise."

"It's Dandelion. Dandelion Greene." I held my breath waiting for a chortle, a giggle, a suppressed snort. "Jade got the last decent green name and my mother thought it was fun to take the naming thing in a whole new direction. Whenever I complain she reminds me she could have named me Beet."

"Or Collard. I think Dandelion suits you," he said. That was something I'd never heard before.

"I don't like to think of myself as an unwelcomed weed."

"That's not what I meant." He took my face in his

hands and tilted it toward his. "Do you know what I always think when I see dandelions?"

"Someone needs to get out the mower?"

"I always think of them as wish flowers because of the way kids make wishes on them." Graham bent and kissed me on the tip of my nose. "I still wish on them every chance I get. Know what I wished for all last summer?"

"No," I said, my heart catching in my throat.

"A Dandelion just like you." I squeezed his hand and we didn't do much talking for quite a long time.

Thirty-two

Piper caught my arm as soon as I came through the door of the Stack. She steered me not to my favorite booth near the back of the restaurant but to the oversize storage closet next to the kitchen.

"Spill," she said as soon as she'd closed the door behind us.

"It was Priscilla who took the money and who killed Spooner." I had just been at the police station giving my official statement to Lowell and had gone over everything with Myra and Mitch sitting there goggle-eyed. My patience with the story was at its end.

"I know all about that. Hazel was already in giving all the juicy details." That figured. I'd stopped in at Greener Pastures first thing to tell the family what had happened before any of them heard about it secondhand.

And I'd spent some time checking in on the sugaring

operation. Nothing made me feel like everything was right with the world like being out in the sugar bush. Hazel must have hustled over to town to share what she knew while I was busy working. "I mean about the fact that you ought to look utterly done in after last night. Instead, you're all glowy."

"I don't know what you're talking about." The words squeaked out through my pursed lips.

"If you don't want to tell me I'll just have to guess." Piper looked me up and down like I was a fifteen-year-old she had just caught sneaking in three hours past curfew. "You haven't had time to change your hair. That isn't a new outfit."

"I got a surprisingly good night's sleep, considering." Which was true. I had enjoyed the best night's sleep I'd had in ages, even with the snoring in my ear.

"That's it then." Piper winked at me. The fluorescent lighting glinted off the silver hoop piercing her eyebrow. "And there I was thinking I would be the first sleepover guest at your new apartment."

"Then I guess you should have been the one braving the storm last night to see how I was."

"Hazel didn't mention that part," Piper said.

"I thought telling the family about the close call with Priscilla was as much excitement as they could take all at once. Besides, it isn't really anyone's business but mine and Graham's."

"You just keep telling yourself that." Piper popped the door open. "I've got to get back to work. If you want to fill me in on the details later I'll be all ears. If not,

I'll know you think he's a keeper. Either way, I'm happy for you." With that, she headed back to the restaurant floor. I followed her and spotted Tansey sitting at the counter looking like her usual self.

"Well there's the woman of the hour." Tansey patted the stool next to her. I looked around for Knowlton. I wasn't sure I was up to being sandwiched between the two of them. He was nowhere in sight so I climbed up onto the stool and prepared for the onslaught.

"Nice to see that you're feeling well enough to come to town, Tansey."

"I am now," Tansey said, dropping her voice. "Thanks to you." Tansey reached over and patted me on the back. I felt the threat of tears starting to spring to my eyes.

It might have been from the force of Tansey's hand thumping my shoulder blade but it was probably how touched I felt by her uncharacteristic show of affection. Tansey isn't a physically demonstrative person. I've never even seen her hug Knowlton. I took a deep breath to steady my voice before swiveling my stool in her direction.

"I guess this means I've upheld my end of the bargain and that you'll be back to full duties on the festival committee, right?" I asked.

"The way I remember it was that if you didn't help clear Spooner's name I was not going to be able to help with the festival anymore. I don't remember saying that if you did I would come out of retirement." Piper appeared in front of us with a paper bag and handed it to Tansey, who elbowed me in the ribs then walked out of the Stack whistling.

*   *   *

When I was growing up we collected sap in buckets instead of using tubing strung between the trees. When my great-great-grandfather was a child they boiled the sap down in cauldrons hung over fires built in clearings in the woods. One thing that hasn't changed over the years is the fun of an old-time sugaring off party just for family and friends.

We pull out the cauldrons and the ladles and the family heirloom wooden buckets. We don our winter woolens and mark the calendar for a full day of hauling sap by a horse-drawn cart and boiling it down over an open flame. Everyone participates and everyone has a great time. It's like Thanksgiving and a family camping trip all rolled into one. Even Celadon seems to love it.

In all the excitement of the preparations I was able to forget the troubles of the last few days. Loden, Clark, and Graham did the heavy lifting with the cauldron under Grampa's expert guidance. Celadon and Piper packed hot, freshly fried batches of cider doughnuts into towel-lined baskets and carried them into the woods.

I couldn't help but notice how Piper broke off a piece of doughnut and laughingly popped it into Loden's mouth. His hand reached up to touch hers and I felt a flicker of hope for the two of them. Graham caught me noticing them and gave me a wink that let me know he was thinking the same thing.

Grandma stood over a small cast-iron kettle patiently checking a batch of syrup she was boiling down to make sugar on snow. Spring and Hunter stood beside her at the ready to test the candy for doneness. Sugar on snow has got to be about as old as sugaring itself. All you need is some syrup and a patch or a pan of clean snow. Once you've boiled some finished syrup down to the soft-ball stage, about 233 degrees Fahrenheit, you ladle it out quickly onto a swath of clean snow.

Sometimes it takes a few tries to get it just right but no one minds sampling the candy until Grandma says she's satisfied. Because it is so sweet Grandma always serves dill pickles along with the candy. It may sound strange but it's well worth a try.

My mother and Lowell stood next to each other, laughing as they poured sap from wooden pails into the cauldron. Even Hazel took a break from stirring up trouble. She sat on a stump near the fire with a cigar clamped between her teeth but in a spirit of goodwill and cooperation she hadn't lit it. She was heading home the next day and the thought occurred to me that she was trying to leave on a sweet note.

Jade, surrounded by billowing clouds of sweet-smelling steam, looked like she was enjoying herself. The weak winter sunlight glinted off the perfect sheen of her blond hair and for the first time in years I was glad she was there instead of wishing she wasn't.

Celadon crunched her way across the packed-down snow to stand beside me. Her cheeks were rosy and her nose was red but her eyes were bright and sparkling.

"When we're all here together, doing something like this, I can't help but feel like the luckiest person in the world," I said as I pointed at all the happy activity surrounding us. She took a step forward and wrapped her parka-swaddled arms around me. "What was that for?"

"Because I admire your attitude. A lot of people would still be in bed with the covers pulled over their heads after what you've been through lately. Me included." Celadon never said things like that. Worry clutched at my chest.

"Is this your way of telling me you need one of my kidneys?"

"It's my way of saying I appreciate how the way you live your life reminds me to be my best self even when I'd rather be an uptight grump." Celadon squeezed my mittened hand with one of her own before leaving me to join her children in tasting a fresh batch of maple candy.

Standing a little apart from the group, watching them smiling, jostling, laughing, and boiling sap my heart swelled in my chest. Almost everyone I loved was together and flourishing. Only one was missing. And then, out of the corner of my eye I could have sworn I caught a glimpse of my father leaning up against a maple tree covering his eyes like he was playing a game of hide-and-seek with me the way he used to when I was small.

Maybe, just maybe, my mother was right and he'd been trying to get in touch with me all along. I decided not to look too closely, not to break the spell. Things were perfectly sweet just the way they were.

Recipes

Maple Pumpkin Butter

This fills your kitchen with a perfect autumnal scent as it slowly simmers. It tastes as good as it smells spread on crisp toast or used as a filling between layers of cake. Or beat some together with softened cream cheese and use as a dip for pretzels.

30 ounces canned pumpkin puree
⅓ cup maple syrup
1 ¼ cups brown sugar
1 teaspoon cinnamon
½ teaspoon ground ginger
¼ teaspoon nutmeg
⅛ teaspoon ground cloves
⅛ teaspoon cardamom

Spray a slow cooker with nonstick cooking spray. In a bowl combine all ingredients and add to the slow cooker. Cook on low setting for 6 hours, or until mixture is reduced to a thickened, spreadable consistency.

Bacon Maple Chutney

This makes a wonderful housewarming gift or something nice to have on hand in the fridge when guests happen to drop by.

1 pound bacon
3 cups thinly sliced sweet onions
¼ cup maple syrup
3 sprigs fresh rosemary
freshly cracked black pepper, to taste

In a large skillet, fry bacon until crisp. Remove from pan. Remove and reserve 2 tablespoons melted bacon fat from skillet and discard the rest. Return pan to burner and add reserved fat. Reduce heat to low and add onions and sprigs of rosemary, cooking slowly and stirring occasionally until they are very soft and golden in color. Chop bacon into small pieces and add to the pan. Stir in the maple syrup and continue stirring until it is reduced and the entire mixture is sticky and thickened. Remove rosemary sprigs. Add cracked pepper to taste. Serve with crackers and cheese or add to sandwiches.

Salted Maple Cream Pie

This delicious treat goes together quickly with very few ingredients. If you're pressed for time it's even yummy if you use a store-bought, prebaked crust. Go ahead, Piper will never know!

1 ½ cups pure maple syrup (Grade B is best for a
    richer maple flavor)
1 cup half-and-half or heavy cream
½ cup all-purpose flour
½ cup water
¼ teaspoon salt
⅛ teaspoon ground nutmeg
1 prebaked piecrust, either homemade or
    store-bought

In a saucepan whisk together the maple syrup, salt, nutmeg, and cream. In a separate bowl whisk together the water and the all-purpose flour until no lumps remain. Heat the maple syrup/cream mixture over medium heat until it begins to steam. Slowly whisk in the flour/water mixture. Stir constantly over medium-high heat until it starts to boil and thickens, about three minutes.

Pour into piecrust and cool to room temperature. Place in the refrigerator and chill until completely cold. Serve with a dollop of whipped cream.

WELL-CRAFTED MYSTERIES FROM BERKLEY PRIME CRIME

- **Earlene Fowler** Don't miss these Agatha Award–winning quilting mysteries featuring Benni Harper.

- **Monica Ferris** These *USA Today* bestselling Needlecraft Mysteries include free knitting patterns.

- **Laura Childs** Her Scrapbooking Mysteries offer tips to satisfy the most die-hard crafters.

- **Maggie Sefton** These popular Knitting Mysteries come with knitting patterns and recipes.

- **Lucy Lawrence** These brilliant Decoupage Mysteries involve cutouts, glue, and varnish.

- **Elizabeth Lynn Casey** The Southern Sewing Circle Mysteries are filled with friends, southern charm—and murder.

M5G0610